PRAIRIE FIRE

Gary Repetto

TotalRecall Publications, Inc.
1103 Middlecreek
Friendswood, Texas 77546
281-992-3131 281-482-5390 Fax
www.totalrecallpress.com

ISBN: 978-1-59095-498-0
UPC: 6-43977-44980-1

Library of Congress Control Number: 2015951367

Printed in the United States of America with simultaneous printing in
Australia, Canada, and United Kingdom.

FIRST EDITION
1   2   3   4   5   6   7   8   9   10

*To my dear wife Antoinette
and our wonderful children,
Danette, Christopher and Cheryl*

Author Bio

Gary Repetto is a former high school all-star football player who played and coached in big time college football. He was also the commissioner of a state wide youth football program, his responsibilities including the interviewing, hiring and overseeing of coaches for a 2000 player organization. After coaching he became a corporate recruiter, recruiting and hiring several thousand engineers in the defense and mining industries over a long, successful career. Working on his second novel, he lives in Arizona with his wife, Antoinette and their family.

Visit with Gary at: www.garyrepetto.com

About The Book

Four teenagers, one the star quarterback of his high school's team, their fathers and their coach plus a corrupt college booster and a police captain, collide with greed, ambition and convoluted definitions of morally right.

This book takes place in 1958 at a Catholic high school in Chicago where the game of football is extremely competitive and among the best in the country. It wasn't uncommon for a school to have 5 to 10 players receive major college scholarships and coaches to be snapped up by colleges throughout the country. This environment is the backdrop for this book in which Mike Bonjanovich is possibly the best quarterback in the country, but he is also a mean, hateful, vindictive individual. His presence almost insures his school, Malloy High School, will win the coveted city championship which would present sought after opportunities for a number of people. But his part in a tragic accidental death of 3 boys witnessed by a freshman student creates several conflicts that reveal a win-at-all-costs attitude by many. The story moves quickly to a dramatic conclusion with good finally overcoming evil. Secondary to the conflict this story reveals life as a student in an inter-city Catholic high school in Chicago during the 1950's (and into the early to mid-1960's)

Preface

This is essentially a book of good versus evil. The cause of the fire was accidental and the two high school senior football players would have likely been reprimanded at worst if they had been forthcoming about unintentionally setting the fire, in addition to not running from the scene. But the arrogance and duplicity of the quarterback, Bonjanovich, and the foolishness of the center, Costello, in trying to protect his quarterback lends to a much greater crime with far reaching consequences. Because of these severe aftereffects good becomes very difficult in overcoming evil.

Prolog
Fall 1958

A desolate prairie stretched across three city lots in the middle of a neighborhood of Chicago's far west side. No one would guess that three small boys would lose their lives tragically that morning in this prairie of rocks and weeds.

Prairies were commonplace in the growing city at this time as land was plentiful. They might be an open lot where a house will be built, or a sizable parcel of land large enough for a factory to be constructed. Later, the prairies would disappear when homes and businesses took their place and land became expensive. But at this time they were common and children often played in them. Parks were generally a bit far for the smaller boys and girls to venture to, so they sought out a nearby prairie. They weren't pretty, mind you. Weeds and rocks galore and broken bottles most anywhere you looked. But children thrived on them. Ball diamonds were devised. Football fields were marked out if the dimensions allowed. Forts were built. Youngsters loved forts. They could be simple, perhaps just a cardboard box. Or they could be well constructed of wood or maybe metal if the boys were especially industrious. In the winter discarded Christmas trees made a snug fort with the pleasant fragrance of pine needles.

On this particular Saturday fall morning the air was blistery with a sharp chilly wind from the north causing golden leaves to swirl up in circles like little tornadoes. Two boys of high school age were wasting the day away throwing rocks in this prairie. They threw rocks at most anything at all. They broke wooden boards, smashing them against the hard ground. They were both big boys for their age, with one bigger than the other. Bored with this pointless activity, they looked to do something perhaps a bit more menacing. Then the shortest of the pair spotted a boy walking toward an alley to the side of the prairie. He was weighted down to a side by a large book bag strapped to his right shoulder.

"Look who's there," he said. "You recognize that kid?"

The taller boy smiled and picked up a smooth stone that fit well in his large hand and threw it hard at the boy who was several years younger than the pair. The stone whizzed true through the air past the boy's ear and crashed loudly off a nearby steel garbage can causing the boy to jump with alarm. Instinctively, he broke into a run up the alley, leaning far forward to compensate for the weight of book bag on his side.

The two boys laughed rowdily and hurled more stones until their victim was out of range. Angry that they hadn't at least hit the boy, they looked for other targets.

"See that fort over there," the bigger boy said. "I'll bet you can't hit it."

The structure was made of oil-slicked forms used to hold poured concrete for new buildings. The fort was well engineered against a brick building wall at the end of the prairie. The other boy clenched his teeth as if a major challenge had come his way and picked up stone and threw it wildly to the side.

"Ha!" the taller one reproached the other. "Try a shingle," he said pointing at a pile of smoldering roof shingles nearby that were likely from a fire started by a neighbor to perhaps get rid of junk from home.

Smarting from humiliation the boy picked up a shingle and

sailed it toward the fort. A trail of smoke followed the piece of tar as it fell to the ground like a wounded quail. The larger boy laughed callously and the other picked up another and threw it hard but with the same result. He fumed as the taller boy laughed even louder.

"It's not that easy. You try it."

"I will and I'll hit it," he said picking up a shingle with a good glow on it. He eyed the fort, a good fifty yards away, and flung the shingle with great force. It sailed true and remained true and then fell atop the oiled boards.

"Bulls Eye," he bragged. "You couldn't do that, you little shrimp."

"It was a lucky throw," the other said. "And don't call me that."

Admiring his accurate toss he was about to add something when a flame flashed up from the fort.

"Wow! Look at that!" the shorter boy shouted as the oil on the boards caught fire and spread with fierce intensity, quickly engulfing the wood structure.

They turned to run when the shorter of the two said, "Did you hear that? It sounds like someone is yelling from the fort!"

The other grabbed his friend by the collar of his jacket and said, "I didn't hear anything. Let's go before someone calls the cops."

They took off in a sprint toward the alley up which the younger boy with the book bag had run a few moments earlier. But just before entering it, the smaller boy stopped to look back. Only for a second, though, as the other again took him by the collar and they continued to run as sirens began to be heard in the distance.

Chapter 1

The city bus was moving east along North Avenue much slower than Andrew Sikorski had anticipated it would on his very first day at Archbishop Malloy High School. Located on Chicago's Westside, the prominent Catholic school was approximately a forty-five minute ride from Andrew's house in Oak Park, the childhood home of Hemingway and several well-known mobsters.

A sound mathematician, and just an overall bright young boy, Andrew had timed the route precisely during the past two weeks to eliminate the slightest chance that he might be late. But late he was becoming on this unseasonably sultry morning for early September. In the past weeks, he had taken several dry runs, picking up the Oak Park bus a couple of blocks from his home and changing to the Chicago bus at the city limits. All trials were during the morning rush hour. Using a slide rule, he considered an extra half an hour for the increase in passengers from four high schools along the way, all of which began classes on this same morning. Checking the enrollment of each school, he devised a formula to estimate the number of additional riders along the route. Amazingly, he was quite close with his calculations, but he had failed to take into account the time spent of boys harassing girls, as one of the schools was a Catholic girl's academy. Dressed in plaid uniform skirts and white blouses, they were the center of attention of the rowdy public school boys. "Can I help you up the steps?" a boy would ask, offering a hand and a smile. "Can I help you off?" one would dramatically suggest. The girls acted as if they were offended by the shenanigans, but they would then smile covertly. All of this took time; time that was turning Andrew into a basket case.

"Please hurry!" he pleaded to the bus driver from his front row seat. "I'm late!"

"You'll get there, kid", the sweaty driver said as he turned the large wheel to swing the bus back out into traffic from a previous stop. Rings showed under his armpits and a kerchief, tied at the neck, was already wet. It would be a very hot day.

Behind Andrew were two scruffy boys who seemed to be quite carefree.

"You're going to get expelled," one taunted Andrew, elbowing his friend. "Expelled, expelled, expelled," the other laughed, making a goofy face.

Andrew ignored them.

"Come to the lake with us," the first said. "You're late already. It won't matter."

"We'll be swimming like all the fishes," the second chirped pursing his lips open and closed like a fish with large round eyes.

Andrew continued to ignore them, but they had diverted his attention from the route. He looked at a street sign and yelled to the driver, "You missed my stop!"

"You got to ring the bell, kid," the driver yelled.

"But you missed my stop! It was Latrobe, and I'm right here by the door," Andrew cried out with anguish as the two kids acting like morons behind him rolled with laughter.

"He missed his stop at Latrobe," one mimicked, punching his brethren in the arm.

"Hey, don't hit me so hard," the boy yelled, rubbing the arm.

Meanwhile, Andrew pulled down and held the cord that signaled a stop and the driver called out to him, "Let go or I take you past the next stop, kid."

"This is intolerable," Andrew yelled back.

"Intolerable," one of the boys said with wide eyes and a crooked head.

The other stuck his tongue out to the side and shook his head. "Intolerable!"

They laughed and punched each other on the arms.

Finally, Andrew got off the bus two streets past his stop and started to run back awkwardly with his heavy book bag bruising his side while the two morons made faces from a bus window.

At that moment, two blocks ahead on Latrobe another tardy boy was walking toward the school, but at a much more casual pace. Tony Barbini was enjoying a smoke as he gazed up at the broad oak leaves of the trees that shaded the street. Eisenhower was president and the world was just fine, he pondered. Tony was a freshman like Andrew, but there any similarity ended. Taller, with brown hair, he kept the required Malloy dress tie waded in his hip pocket, and he carried no textbooks. Incorrigible is how nuns from the various grade schools he had attended fondly described Tony. They would rap him on the head with their knuckles, but they then gushed over him as well. Tony had enjoyed his grade school days, and he was sure he would take pleasure in Malloy, seeing that his dear mother had begged and pleaded for the school to take him in. But he was in no hurry to begin this coming joy. He took one last drag on the cigarette and flicked it into the street when a voice gruffly shouted at him.

"Hey kid, you got some smokes for us?"

Tony turned and saw two older boys sitting on a bench in a gangway by a small candy store. They were both strong athletic looking boys.

"Sure," Tony replied obligingly.

He went to them and shook out a few cigarettes from his package of Lucky Strikes. The one who had called out, a muscular boy with dark features, took the entire package from Tony's hand.

"Didn't your mother tell you you're too young to smoke? It'll stunt your growth."

The other, shorter than the first, but a strong boy also, snickered and said, "That's good Mike. If he doesn't grow any more, he'll be a midget." The boy quickly looked to Mike for a reaction to his wit and was disappointed that there was none.

"That wasn't very nice. I offered you my cigarettes and you did that," Tony said.

"Hey you," the smaller said. "You getting smart with Mike and me?"

"No," Tony replied. "It's not a big deal. I'm just telling you that wasn't very nice."

"Maybe it is a big deal," the boy said, watching Mike from the corner of his eye. "Let's kick his ass, Mike." He closed his hands into fists and stood up from the bench.

Mike remained seated, watching Tony with amusement.

"You're late on your first day and you're pissing Johnny off. You're not very smart are you?"

Tony shrugged his shoulders. "I'd better get going," he said.

"Here, let me give you one of your smokes back," Mike offered.

"No, keep them."

"I insist."

Before Tony could turn to leave, Mike took a cigarette from the pack, then crushed the remaining smokes in his fingers, allowing the tobacco to fall to the ground.

Johnny hooted with his hands to his stomach and sat back down.

"Very funny," Tony said as he turned and left.

The two boys watched him walk away.

"I don't like him, Mike. We should have kicked his ass."

"He's a punk," Mike said.

"Well, we'll watch for him in school," Johnny stated and was disappointed again when Mike only grunted.

CHAPTER 2

Perhaps if the two freshmen had not been late on that first morning, or if Tony had not been delayed by Mike and Johnny, or if Andrew had taken an earlier bus, the lives of all four boys might have turned out differently. Who can tell about fate? As it was, Tony and Andrew arrived at the front door of Malloy High School at the same time, both very late. Tony held the door for the blonde boy with perfectly parted straight hair.

"Late too, huh?" Tony said.

Andrew was not about to partake in chitchat and ran by Tony without as much as a 'thank you'. Tony jogged and caught up with the boy in the empty hallway.

"Boy, you sure got a lot of books," he said, watching Andrew struggle along at a near run. "Need some help?"

"No. I just need to get to my class."

"Which one you going to?"

"B-10. It's in the basement. But I must go to my locker first."

"B-10! That's my class too. I'll go to your locker with you. I don't have any books."

The cavalier attitude of this boy reminded Andrew distressingly of the two ingrates on the bus, and he wanted nothing to do with him. "No. You go ahead."

"Nonsense," Tony said. "I can't let you go in later than me. You'll get crucified."

Andrew was in too much of a hurry to ask what he meant, but the comment bothered him.

Having deposited his books in his locker, Andrew hurried to the classroom. Tony was amazed that the boy knew precisely where his locker was located in addition to the location of their first class. He had absolutely no idea where to find his locker or the class. He hadn't even been sure where Malloy was located.

"How do you know where everything is?" Tony asked, mystified.

"I simulated my first day two weeks ago," he answered hurriedly. He had said more than he wanted to the boy.

"Simulated? You're kidding!" Tony thought a second and said. "You actually wasted a summer day coming here when you didn't have to?"

Andrew didn't answer him. Upon arriving at their classroom, Andrew reached for the doorknob, but Tony stopped him.

"What's wrong?" Andrew exclaimed with dismay.

"We don't have a plan."

"A plan! What are talking about?"

"Look at that teacher," Tony said, pointing to a hefty priest with a chubby face. There was nothing friendly about his appearance as he jawed at frightened students. Though the closed door muffled the priest's voice, it was intimidating to Andrew. On the blackboard behind the teacher was his name in large letters 'FATHER CHESTER SADAK'!!!!! Several thick exclamation marks followed the name.

Andrew hesitated a moment, then said, "We're wasting time."

Tony again restrained Andrew's hand on the doorknob. "What will you tell him?"

"I'll tell him what happened," Andrew answered impatiently.

"Which is?"

"The bus was late!"

"Oh, no!" Tony said disparagingly. "Chicago buses are never late."

"But it's the truth."

Tony shook his head with his lips pursed. "It won't work. Now do you have a brother?"

Andrew hesitated, and then said, "Yes, but...."

He cut Andrew off. "Pay attention. Your brother was afraid to go to school alone on his first day. Your parents are working, so you had to take him. Remember that he goes to a Catholic school. You won't get much sympathy if it's a public school."

"But I can't lie like that."

Tony pointed to the priest. "See that face. He's not in a good mood. If you don't have a good explanation, he'll hurt you."

"What do you mean hurt me?" Andrew exclaimed, genuinely horrified. "A teacher wouldn't hurt me! That's unheard of!"

Tony draped his arm around Andrew's shoulder in a brotherly manner. "This isn't grade school where the nuns rap your knuckles. These guys will wallop you."

Andrew watched Father Sadak ranting about something with a piece of chalk in his hand. His black cassock was already marred white from chalk dust. He didn't look friendly at all.

"But..."

"No buts. Just say that! Believe me, it'll work."

Surrendering, the boy nodded and adjusted the books in his arm. He just wanted in the classroom.

"Okay," Tony said and opened the door.

Father Sadak abruptly stopped his ranting and turned

toward the interruption, leaning forward with his hands on his hips. As one, the heads of the freshmen students rotated toward the late boys. There was complete silence as Father Sadak moved toward Tony and Andrew still with his hands on his hips.

"Do you two know what time it is?"

"We're a little late, Father," Tony apologized.

"A little late! Two minutes is a little late." He looked up at the clock on the wall. "Twenty minutes isn't late, it's missing the class. Why did you even bother showing up?"

The priest leaned slightly forward. "What are your names?"

"I'm Tony Barbini," Tony answered somewhat cheerfully. "And this is…"

"Let him answer!" he boomed as Tony realized that he didn't know the boy's name anyhow.

"Andrew Sikorski, Father," Andrew said in fretfully timid voice.

"I can't hear you! Speak up."

"Andrew Sikorski," he answered maybe a decibel higher.

"What?" the priest bellowed, turning an ear for effect.

"Andrew Sikorski!" the boy sobbed.

The priest leaned back and folded his arms.

"Okay, now that we know who you are, pray tell, why are you two late? You first, Mr. Sikorski."

Andrew fought the tears back and had to swallow a couple of times to get a voice. He could only think of the excuse Tony had proposed. He glanced toward him and then said unsteadily, "My father was working and I had to take my brother to school."

"Oh," the priest said looking out to his audience of students, "and what about your mother?"

He looked down at the floor to keep his eyes away from the priest.

"Look at me!" he chided abruptly, and Andrew jerked his head back up.

"She's dead," he said softly, looking away.

Father Sadak nodded. He was in no mood to offer sympathy.

"I see. And what grade is your brother in?"

Andrew didn't answer.

"Come on now, Mr. Sikorski, it's very simple. Just how old is your brother? That will tell us what grade he's in."

Andrew wiped his eyes underneath the glasses. He had never before lied to an adult, let alone a priest, and he was sick of doing so again.

"He's twenty-four."

The class broke into laughter, but was quickly silenced by a glare from the priest. His angry eyes returned to the boy.

"So you deliberately lied to me?"

Andrew nodded, "I'm sorry."

With his hands on his hips, Father Sadak bent down so that his face was close to Andrew's. His breath reeked of stale cigarette tobacco, unlike the sweet pipe tobacco aroma around Andrew's father.

"That's quite a story. Did you make it up yourself or did someone help you with it?" He looked behind the boy at Tony sensing he was the roguish one, and returned his intense stare to Andrew. "Well Mr. Sikorski, we don't have all day. Did someone, perhaps your friend here, prompt you to tell such a story?"

Andrew didn't want to answer, but he couldn't tell the priest another lie.

"Well!" he bellowed so that Andrew jumped back into Tony.

Unable to take any more, he cried, "Yes, he did." A finger went partially up in the direction of Tony.

The priest nodded and eased back.

"Okay, Mr. Sikorski. You can take a seat. I'll figure out a proper punishment for you later."

Struggling with the schoolbooks against his chest, he looked straight at the floor and moved quickly to an empty desk in at the rear of the class. Father Sadak turned his attention to Tony while the class waited in silent and fearful anticipation.

"So, you're not just satisfied with causing trouble for yourself. You have to bring misery to others also." He waited for effect, and then asked, "And what is your name, again?"

"Tony Barbini."

"Tony Barbini, what?" The priest barked.

Tony shrugged, "Just Tony Barbini. I don't use a middle name."

The class snickered, but went silent with another glare from their teacher.

"It's Tony Barbini, Father! You're not in some public school, Mr. Barbini!"

"Tony Barbini, Father," he complied.

The priest shook his head and a deceitful smile crossed his face.

"You are not starting on the right foot, Mr. Barbini. Is there a particular reason you decided to waste a valuable space at Malloy?"

"I really wanted to go to Madonna, Father, but they

wouldn't let a boy in the school," Tony joked, referring to a nearby girl's school.

The class of fourteen-year old boys roared in unison and again became silent after a gasp when the priest cuffed Tony hard on the side of his head with an open palm.

"Don't you blaspheme the school of the Holy Mother!"

The blow stung, but Tony didn't waiver. He figured he'd better not say anything more lest he might get one square in the face.

"You're a disgrace, Mr. Barbini, and you shouldn't be here with these good boys," the priest yelled. "Get out in the hall now and kneel." He went to the door and held it open. "I said now!"

Tony hustled through the door and got down on his knees on the marble floor.

"Get your back straight and your arms out in front of you," Father Sadak said stepping out into the hallway.

Tony straightened up and extended his arms slightly as if they were stubs. Losing patience, the priest grabbed the boy's arms and yanked them. "Straight out! I don't want your elbows bent. And the arms better not drop below your shoulders. Do you understand?" he yelled.

Tony nodded.

"What?" He cocked his ear close to Tony's face for emphasis.

"I understand, Father."

The priest returned to his classroom and slammed the door shut. He watched Tony from the window for several moments and then disappeared from view.

Tony looked down the quiet hallway and sighed. It wasn't the first time he had been sent to the hall to kneel. But at least the floors in the old grade school buildings had been made of wood and were easier on the knees. This was marble and would become hard on him very fast. He rocked back and forth to ease the weight from his knees. Then he inched up near the wall. Pretty soon he'd be leaning against the wall to take the pressure from his back. Then he'd fall back on his haunches to help his knees. Tony knew the ropes. But he wouldn't be in the hall long enough for any adjustments, for in less than a minute another priest came down the stairs. He was moving with purpose.

"What are you doing out here?" the priest asked sternly.

Tony sensed that he shouldn't wisecrack with this one whose eyes meant business through wire-rimmed glasses.

"Father told me to kneel for the rest the class."

"Why?"

"I was late and I guess I made up a story."

"You lied?"

"Yes, kind of."

"What is your name?"

"Tony Barbini."

"Get up," he ordered and opened the door to the class.

"Father, take this boy back into class so that he doesn't get behind on the first day. Have him come to my office after school."

Father Sadak smugly stated, "He shouldn't be a Malloy student, Father Principal. And there's another one just like him."

"Have him come to my office also."

The principal held the door for Tony to return, and then left.

"Take a seat in the back somewhere where I don't have to look at you," the priest said with obvious disdain that the impudent boy was before him again. Tony complied. He found a seat in the rear next to Andrew Sikorski who closed his eyes in anguish.

"Don't worry about telling on me, Andy," Tony whispered from the side of his mouth. "I shouldn't have put you on the spot."

Andrew shook his head and dropped it between his arms on the desk. He hated the name Andy.

CHAPTER 3

On the first day of classes the lunch periods were typically hectic and quite confusing to the freshmen. Unfamiliar with the procedure, the younger boys formed bottlenecks at the lunchroom entrance and at various stops along the counter line. And they had no idea of the unwritten seating rules. Scheduled for the first lunch period were the freshmen and senior classes combined. A priority with any large gathering at the high school was to discourage disorder. Sophomores commonly harass freshmen and seniors sometimes have a dislike for juniors. Sophomores occasionally mix poorly with juniors, but seniors seldom have any problems with freshmen. For several years now the seniors ate with the freshman while the sophomores ate with juniors. The mixed period didn't really mean that the two classes would eat together, of course, as a freshman would be entirely out-of-place eating at a senior's table. Freshmen tables were separate and comprised about two-thirds of the lunchroom. It wasn't a perfect arrangement, but it worked relatively well.

Seated at one table along the isle of the senior section were three members of the Malloy football team. Two of the three were Mike and Johnny from the candy store, and the other was Al Wasko. At this table, even with a crowded lunchroom, no other students sat; not even other senior classmates and certainly no freshmen. Wasko was the team's fullback. He had a long muscled neck and a pronounced nose, which had been broken several times. Johnny Costello, the center, was short for a lineman in the Chicago Catholic Conference, but he spent much of his time lifting weights at home to make up for his height and had a self-imposed mean and bulldog look to him. Alongside Johnny, and never far from the center's thoughts, was the great quarterback, Mike Bonjanovich. His fame stretched far from the halls of Malloy, as he was well known to anyone in Chicago that was interested in football. As did Andrew, Bonjanovich lived in Oak Park. His home was frequented regularly by college scouts. Former players themselves, many were quite surprised that they were not a match to Mike physically. He was a man among boys. He could easily pass for a college senior rather than a high school student.

"Look at these freshmen," Costello said, nudging his quarterback.

"Yeah, so?" Bonjanovich said biting into a sausage sandwich to which he had helped himself from the center's lunch bag. Johnny's mother made sure that her boy would not starve and thus loaded his lunch bag amply. And he was pleased that the great quarterback chose to take from his lunch bag and was always accommodating.

"They're wimpy," Johnny said, discouraged that his gibe hadn't received the approval he had hoped for from Mike.

"Of course they're wimpy, they're piss-ant freshmen. You were wimpy then."

"No, I wasn't. Maybe Al was, but not me," he taunted, hoping for a laugh.

"You think I was wimpy," Wasko said with a half-full mouth. "I'll kick your ass."

"No, you won't," Johnny defended, sticking his chest out automatically.

Bonjanovich kept his attention on the sandwich but let a small smile cross his face. He enjoyed their child-like barbs here in school, but if they would take this nonsense onto his football field, he would promptly kick both of their asses.

Just then Tony Barbini sat down at the end of their table and then reached for Andrew, who was hurrying past, to sit with him. Andrew tried to pull away, but failed and found himself seated across from Tony at the player's table. Andrew realized their folly immediately when he saw the three seniors staring at them.

"What in the hell are you two doing?" Johnny Costello demanded with disbelief that freshmen would sit at their table when other seniors wouldn't even dare to do so. He recognized Tony. "I should have kicked your ass earlier," he said to Tony.

Andrew was more than glad to leave and started to get up but was stopped by Tony's arm. "We're having lunch", Tony said to the center. "This is the lunchroom, isn't it?"

Johnny glanced toward Mike, and then decided to act. He couldn't let this freshman get away with such impudence a second time. He started to move across the table toward Tony when a short stocky brother with a blonde flattop appeared.

"Hello, boys," Brother Vladimir said with his powerful hands clasped behind his back. His smile showed a number of teeth missing. After three years Johnny knew how deceiving the smile of the lunchroom monitor was and immediately sat back.

"Hello Brother," Bonjanovich said cautiously. Though Mike would stand a good foot taller than the brother, he was one of the few people of whom the great athlete was wary.

The brother glanced briefly at the two freshmen, and then turned his attention to the football players. "A good season coming, lads?"

" We're going to win the City Championship, Brother," Costello enthusiastically replied.

Brother Vladimir's eyes dropped down on the center and the smile was gone, causing Costello to squirm.

The brother pointed his right index finger in the air. "Bragging can be the fuel for the enemy's fire. Isn't that right boys?"

"Yes, Brother, you're right," Costello agreed readily, hoping he hadn't upset the unpredictable Vladimir.

The smile returned. The brother nodded and patted Costello on the head.

"It's a valuable thought that will come in handy someday on the field of battle."

The three senior players all agreed and expressed a drummed up enthusiasm for Brother Vladimir's silly bit of wisdom.

The brother turned to the freshmen and said, "I'm afraid you are at the wrong table boys. This table is for seniors."

His smile bothered Tony.

"Sure," Tony said as he picked up his tray. Andrew was already up and ready to leave.

"Ah, ha," the brother said with a finger again pointed upward. "Sure? Is sure a proper sentence or even worse, a proper sign of respect?" The smile remained, but the little dark eyes narrowed.

From the side Tony could feel the seniors silently gloat and realized that other students nearby had become completely silent.

"No it's not, Brother. I should have said, 'Yes we will, Brother.'" Then he added, "That's why we decided to sit with the seniors, Brother. We don't know the ropes and figured we could learn by watching."

Vladimir waited a moment, seemingly uncertain as to which path to take. Then a safer smile came to his face.

"Yes, perhaps that is wise young man. And what's your name?"

"Tony Barbini, Brother."

"And your name?" he asked Andrew.

"Andrew Sikorski, Brother," the boy answered, disturbed that he had to provide his name in an unfavorable situation for the second time that morning.

"Yes, I will remember you boys. For now, let's get back with your fellow freshmen where you can teach each other good deeds."

They left quickly to find a table with freshmen, and the brother returned his attention to the seniors.

"We're never too old to learn, are we boys?"

"Never, Brother," Bonjanovich agreed, now developing a dislike for the wise-ass kid called Barbini for the kind of attention he had brought to him. Then the proctor moved on and when he was a good distance from their table, Al Wasko said under his breath, "What a hand job."

At that very moment the brother turned around and looked at their table with his hands behind his back. Though Vladimir couldn't have possibly heard the comment, Wasko was sure that he was directing his attention at him and he averted his eyes to a spot on the table. Costello, who had snickered at the comment, followed suit. Bonjanovich hadn't been paying attention. Instead he watched Tony, seated at a lunch bench several tables removed along with the kid he recognized from the neighborhood. He would watch for them later.

CHAPTER 4

In Chicago when one spoke of Malloy High School, one was usually talking about football. Winning teams at the west side school stretched back to the 1920's when Bill McCormick, a decorated hero from the Great War with prodigious honors of courage from the French, began to build powerful teams at the newly established Catholic school on Hubbard Street, north of downtown. In 1950 he moved with the school to its West Side location to continue the rich football tradition. A couple of years later he hired a graduate from one of the local colleges to help with the team. Until then he had only needed an injured player or two for any assistance. But a hip that was about gone and a lung condition required more support than a student was able to give. Frank O'Brien was an excellent coach in the old man's eyes, even though he might have been a little more ambitious for someone just out of school than McCormick would have preferred. But that was all right, he figured. O'Brien was young and a little piss and vinegar might be good for the team.

In O'Brien's mind, on the other hand, he saw McCormick not as helpful mentor or a savvy leader of young men, but as an old man who had been holding on to a highly desired job far too long. As O'Brien took care of the hard work on the field, McCormick watched over practice from a small director's chair that folded up nicely. O'Brien felt that he wasn't given the credit he deserved, but he wasn't about to leave. The head job at Malloy was the plum of high school football in the city and an ideal stepping-stone to the college ranks. The old man wouldn't be around too much longer, he figured.

However it wasn't health that determined it was time for the old man to go. The great Malloy tradition was in jeopardy. The team had lost five games and failed to make the playoffs for the first time in recent memory. Could McCormick be losing his touch? Was he too old to run the show? This way of thinking became quietly common with the ardent fans that had once worshipped the great coach. Bill McCormick hadn't really planned on retiring just yet, but the vigilant backers of the great football program, known as the Father's Club, felt that it was indeed time, and not without the veiled support of Frank O'Brien. So, in 1955 the old coach turned the reins over to his young assistant. The grateful Father's Club of course gave the old man a customary dinner in the school's gym with a watch as a gift, and then quickly turned their energies to the savior of the Malloy program.

Frank O'Brien didn't disappoint them. Malloy quickly returned to its winning ways, making the playoffs in 1956 and then becoming a contender for the championship. The championship was very important to O'Brien. Several former Catholic Conference coaches were now on the staffs of major colleges, and each had in common at least one city championship. Three years as the head coach at the west side school were enough for him. Much longer and he might be thought of in the same context as McCormick, a very good high school coach who just might remain there for the duration. He was, after all, only the school's second football coach. This was the year to make the move, and a perfect year it was. With the great Bonjanovich at quarterback and a solid team behind him, Malloy was clearly the pre-season favorite for the championship. For the past year nearly every major college football power has been in touch with O'Brien about his quarterback, and he never missed a chance to casually let it be known that he might be open to a good opportunity at a higher level himself.

But Frank O'Brien, a trim man with chiseled features and dark wavy hair, was somewhat uneasy going into the start of this most crucial season. Alone in the small coaches' office with his feet crossed atop an old metal desk, he was dwelling on a disturbing matter that had happened earlier that summer. It was during the Fourth of July weekend that his talented backfield coach, Tom Baker, got drunk and shacked up with a high school junior in Lake Geneva. Word got back to the girl's parents, pillars of a wealthy suburb north of Chicago, and Baker was arrested. With the arrest and the troubling accusations, he was immediately relieved of his teaching and coaching duties by the Malloy principal. O'Brien had tried to talk Father Sobykevich into letting Baker stay on at least until his case went to trial. 'He shouldn't be penalized until found guilty', the coach had argued. 'All sorts of things can happen in this type of a situation. The girl might have lied about her age to Baker. Maybe she made the whole thing up to get some attention. There's no telling what a girl like that is liable to do.' O'Brien tried in vain to sway his principal in hopes that he could hold on to Baker through the season. But the principal would have nothing to do with it. Baker was gone, replaced by an eager young English teacher who didn't know the first thing about football.

The bell announcing the period change jolted him from his thoughts. He pitched a pencil he had been toying with onto the desk and uncrossed his feet and dropped them to the floor. It was time to get to work. His line coach and the English teacher would be there momentarily with only a quarter of an hour remaining to review the practice schedule and dress for the field. Another reason he longed for the college game where a coach was strictly a coach and wasn't required to teach five or six classes before practice. The focus would be completely on football and not a lot of other nonsense.

Just then he heard his line coach's voice from outside the office in the gym. Jack Stone was arguing with the newly assigned backfield coach, Walter Cameron.

"Don't tell me how to coach linemen," Stone snapped back over his shoulder as he stormed into the office. He tossed a textbook onto another metal desk that the two assistants shared. Stone had broad shoulders and stood over six feet. He had a light complexion with short hair trimmed above the ears. Cameron, a thin young man with dark hair, cut longer, followed behind.

"But why don't you just consider my suggestion. It's really a matter of simple physics," Cameron said.

Stone stopped and turned. "Listen, you know what you can do with your physics crap. Besides, last I heard, you're an English teacher."

"Don't be so mulish, Jack. I realize that I haven't had the playing experience that you have had, but most things have generic basics."

Stone put his hands on his hips and stared at the teacher. At first, O'Brien thought that his line coach might smack Cameron. His initial sentiment was to go ahead and let him have a good one right here in the office. But then he could well be without a line coach also and was about to intercede when Stone calmed down.

"Don't call me, Jack," he said quietly, taking his tie off. "It's 'Coach' around here."

Cameron thought on that a moment, and then said, "That's another matter I've given some thought to. Shouldn't we be less formal with the students? I think they will relate better if we're on a first name basis. I know that my English students respond much better when they're allowed to call me Walter."

Stone gritted his teeth stretching his tie in front of Cameron at eye level. "Listen, if I hear any of our players calling you Walter on the field, I'll personally strangle you with this tie in front of the entire team. How's that for response?"

Cameron shook his head but wisely kept quiet as Stone sat heavily on a cushioned chair. When Baker was still on the staff, Jack and he would share this chair accordingly. The other would take a folding metal chair. With Cameron he took sole possession of the chair. The English teacher could sit on the floor for all he cared.

O'Brien handed out the practice schedule.

"We're on the field with the specialists in ten minutes. We'll review it on the way out."

This meant that he and Stone would go over the schedule. Once on the field O'Brien was really the backfield coach with Cameron directed to a singular role of observation.

Stone looked over the schedule while Cameron changed to his coaching gear in the tiny locker area. The English teacher broke into a rendition of 'Some Enchanted Evening' in a rich soprano voice, and Stone plugged his fingers into his ears while continuing to study the schedule.

CHAPTER 5

Fr. John Sobykevich was beginning his third year as principal of Malloy High School. It was an assignment from his order that he had accepted reluctantly, as he had cherished immensely his previous position as Church Historian to the Archdiocese. In the middle of a major work relating to nineteenth century immigration of the clergy from Europe, he was called upon to take over the faltering west side school. Malloy was in a changing neighborhood and the school's enrollment had been declining steadily. At the same time, most quality lay teachers were being lured to the better salaries of the newly emerging suburban schools. Athletics seemed to be the only curriculum not adversely affected by the changes and, though not much of a sports fan himself, he recognized the importance of these activities to the school. Wisely, the principal leveraged the successes of the athletic program to return the school's enrollment in three short years to capacity with a long waiting list. He had his reservations about Frank O'Brien, however. The head coach was indeed successful and the Father's Club, an organization vital to the financial stability of the school, implicitly backed O'Brien. So he guardedly tolerated the ambitious coach.

His dear and devoted secretary, Wanda Black, interrupted his thoughts on this first day of the fall semester.

"You wanted to see this boy, Father," she said in a loud, grating voice. She stood at the principal's doorway with Tony behind her.

"Thank you, Wanda. Please get his file."

"There's another one out here too that's supposed to see you."

"Bring his file also, but have him wait until I'm through with this boy."

"Yes, Father."

She scurried from the office and the principal pointed Tony to a chair and he took it. It was a hard straight chair on a thick carpet. The principal leaned back in a leather chair with his fingers in a steeple on his lap surmising the boy. Wanda returned efficiently with two files and placed them in front of the principal, pointing out Tony's. Father John began to study it carefully.

While the principal was going over his lackluster grade school record, Tony took the opportunity to look around the office. On the wall to the right was a picture of the Pope in a gold frame. On his left were shelves loaded with books and straight ahead behind the principal was a black and white photo of several students around a young priest. All seemed to be enjoying themselves and Tony was quite sure that the priest was the Malloy principal. He decided that he liked this man even though he was about to likely be punished by him.

After a minute or so, Father Sobykevich turned to the other file and spent only a few seconds reviewing it. He put it down and took off his glasses to rub his eyes.

"Is there any particular reason, Mr. Barbini, that you decided to apply to Malloy?"

The freshman shrugged his shoulders. "It really wasn't my idea."

"Whose idea was it?"

"My father's. He's worried about me, I guess."

"I understand why, looking at your record. I see that you attended and were asked to leave several schools, both public and parochial." He tapped his fingers on the file. "Do you realize the number of deserving students we have to turn away each year?"

"I'm very sorry for them, Father," he replied honestly. "I'm afraid they should have been picked over me."

He stared at the boy for several moments, and then asked, "What's your father's name."

"Jack Barbini, Father."

"The police captain?"

"Yes. That's him, Father."

"And your mother, did she want you to come to Malloy also?"

"Not at first, Father. She wanted me to go to Quigley. She thought I should be a priest."

The principal grunted, "And you didn't want to be a priest?"

"Good gosh, no." Then he added, "No offense, Father. But I just don't think I'm cut out for that type of life."

"You are at least astute, Mr. Barbini. And what is it that you feel you might be cut out for?"

Tony thought about that for a moment, then said, "I don't have the slightest idea."

"I suspect that you don't," the priest said and then glanced at the other boy's file. "Did you by chance get Mr. Sikorski into trouble also? He's never done anything wrong in his life."

"Oh yes, I'm glad you brought that up. Andy's a good guy. It was all my fault."

"I figured as much. You will be staying after school for

awhile to help Wanda."

He pushed up from his chair and directed Tony to follow with a crooked finger.

In the main office he addressed his secretary. "Mr. Barbini will be here to help you for the next two weeks." Then he said to Andrew who was waiting anxiously in a chair. "Mr. Sikorski, you're free to go home now and get started with your studies."

Andrew gladly gathered his books and hustled out the door. The principal returned to his office, leaving Tony with the secretary who didn't seem entirely pleased at the prospect of his help.

"Well, Wanda, where should I start?"

"Don't call me Wanda, young man. It's Mrs. Black." She gave a quick glance around and said, "I have to leave early today so just straighten out the copy room and set all the waste baskets out in the hall for Emil to pick up. By tomorrow I'll have a set routine for you."

"That's fine, Ma'am. You can call me Tony."

"Mr. Barbini will do just fine, young man. Now please get busy and let me finish my work."

"Right, Ma'am. You'll be more than pleased with my help and you won't even know I'm here."

"I find that hard to believe, Mr. Barbini," she said

CHAPTER 6

While Tony was just beginning his chores for Wanda, football practice was getting under way a few blocks away at a city park. The afternoon was bright and hot, but the Malloy team had been whipped into shape over the past three weeks and was affected little by the heat. The first day of school meant an end to the grueling two-a-day sessions and the squad was thus in very good spirits. It was also enthused about getting a championship season under way. The coaches were excited, and, of course, the Father's Club was excited. And the prestigious Club was well represented by members at each practice, mostly by fathers of team players. Several would regularly show up on a sideline of the practice field, some ten to fifteen minutes prior to the start of practice to closely observe the progress of their championship team. Men who would have otherwise had little in common rubbed elbows and chatted for those couple of hours as if they were old friends.

"Think they're ready?" one said to another from the side of his mouth.

"Sure they're ready," the other replied with hunched shoulders and his hands in his pockets.

"I just hope they aren't too ready," a third said. He was a salesman of household products. "You can't peak too early in this league."

"They won't peak early," hands-in-pockets said confidently, rocking back and forth on his toes. "O'Brien won't let them."

"I hope your right," the salesman fretted. "I saw it happen to

St. George in the Forties. No one could touch them in the season, and then they lost their first playoff game."

"The North Section was weak that year," the first man who spoke from the side of his mouth, looking straight ahead, said. "St. George had a cake walk through the season."

"They weren't ready for the playoffs."

"I just hope it doesn't happen to us," the salesman said.

It was exciting for these men to follow their sons, the gladiators of Malloy. Plus they had the opportunity to chew the fat with the press and scores of college scouts.

Practice began with a loud enthusiastic cheer from the team after a short pep talk from O'Brien, and then the boys broke into units by position for individual drills. It was a team of substantial talent, and a college scout might be found at any one of the drills. But at this moment the focus was mainly on the quarterback drill. The scouts watched Bonjanovich work his magic. His moves were crisp and smooth and strong. Mike's run-pass option was devastating to a defense. If he chose to pass no high school defender was a match for the remarkable arm, and if he decided to run, he was nearly untouchable. In addition, he was a fierce and powerful runner. He was a grand talent, he was. And he didn't disappoint any this day as the team moved to the scrimmage portion of practice. Bonjanovich was magnificent any time he touched the ball. Thirty, forty yards a clip on his passes. Ten, fifteen, twenty yards every time he carried the ball. And on defense he was a brutal tackler. After four or five fierce tackles, Coach O'Brien replaced him; not from fear of injury to his great quarterback, but from concern of hurting the rest of his team.

It was during a drill later in practice that a nasty incident occurred involving Mike Bonjanovich and Walter Cameron. A slight man, Cameron lifted weights faithfully each day to try to compensate for the delicate body he was given. The barbells did help some as he was able to add a bit of muscle to his frame, but unfortunately he tended to overestimate how much strength he had really gained. In addition, he tended to irritate Bonjanovich to no end.

The backs were working on a 'fill drill' when the English teacher rashly decided to partake and picked up an air bag. It wasn't unusual for the coaches to mix it up with the players. Jack Stone often jumped into drills, sometimes without a blocking dummy or an air bag. But Jack Stone had not long ago played college ball whereas Walter Cameron had not even been selected to an intramural flag football team while in college.

A 'fill drill' requires a lead back to block a defensive player in a tightened space depicting a running corridor while a ball carrier follows behind and cuts away from the block. When Cameron picked up the bag, Al Wasko was in turn to block and Bonjanovich had the ball. Cameron challenged the pair, as a coach might, to drive him from the hole. He taunted them foolishly that they could never block him. It all happened so fast. Wasko slammed a shoulder into the air bag, ripping it from Cameron's hands. The English teacher was left unprotected in the hole with Bonjanovich charging at him at full speed. The ferocious collision caused heads turned from all parts of the practice field. With no intention of cutting off Wasko's block, Bonjanovich had smashed into Cameron head on. The foolish English teacher was rocketed back several yards and landed unconscious on the grass with a wrecked nose that poured blood down over his shirt. Only after being revived with smelling salts was the bleeding stopped by Stone as he administered a dry towel to Cameron's face. It was a matter Father Principal would investigate carefully throughout the week.

CHAPTER 7

That afternoon at a downtown bar above and next to the Chicago River, two men met as if by accident. The older, red-faced with a blue summer suit and a white shirt stretched at the collar, was seated with his back to a large window overlooking the river. Gus Flannigan, a former player at, and now scout for, a major Midwestern university, was somewhat overweight but burly with the type of muscle that never goes away.

"Well for cry-not-loud," he said with raised eyebrows as the other approached with a casual swagger. He rose from the stool to greet him. "Nick, how are you?"

"Fine, Gus, fine," he answered without as much showmanship as they shook hands.

Nick Bonjanovich was a head taller than Gus, and trimmer at the waist. He showed off his arms with a tight knit shirt. Bonjanovich was the father of the great quarterback and the meeting with the college football scout was certainly not by chance.

"Have a drink with me?" Gus offered.

Nick glanced around the bar that opened into a restaurant to one side. At that time in the afternoon the crowd was sparse.

"Sure Gus, I'll join you."

He took a stool next to Gus and ordered a scotch from the bartender. Gus was drinking a martini and he motioned for another.

"How's the kid doing?" Gus asked once they had settled in

with their drinks.

"He's all right," Nick answered with some irritation.

Gus nodded and waited.

"O'Brien better get his coaching staff straightened out," Nick added.

"The coach with the rape charge still out?"

"That Polack principal shouldn't be able to do that. Baker was a good coach. Mike got along with him. This other clown has no business out there."

"I'm sure Frank will take care of things," Gus said. "He's a smart enough guy. And even if things don't work out that well, we all know what Mike can do."

"That's not the point," Nick said as he set an open package of cigarettes on the bar. "Mike wants the championship. This is the year."

He took a cigarette from the pack and offered one to Gus but the college scout declined. Nick lit up and exhaled hard through his nose.

"A damn English teacher who's never played a down of football in his life," Nick said irritably. "How'd O'Brien let him get away with that?"

"It doesn't figure, does it," Gus said before taking a generous drink from the martini. He twirled the remainder around with the ice. "Assuming O'Brien keeps it together, how's the season look?"

"We won't lose a game," Nick stated frankly. "We'll beat every team in the league by three touchdowns."

Gus nodded. "That's saying something in this league. And I believe it." He leaned closer to Nick. "You know how we feel about Mike. With him we can win the national championship, two, maybe three years from now, and you'll just be a couple of hours away. You can see every game and you know we'll take good care of your family."

Having not yet received what he had come for, Nick said nothing and Gus picked up on it. He gave the room a quick once over and reached into a side jacket pocket. Out came a fat sealed envelope. Keeping it below the bar and out of sight, he passed it to Nick, who neatly slipped it under his shirt inside his belt. Even a trained eye might not have recognized the swift exchange.

"This is to show our good faith in Mike," Gus said quietly. "I think you'll be pleased with the amount. Like I said, there'll be plenty more if Mike signs with us."

Nick knocked back the rest of his scotch.

"Thanks, Gus," he said as if it were money owed to him and not the sweetener that it was. "I'll be sure that Mike gets the message." He rose quickly and adjusted the package so that it fit better. "I hate to run, but I've got an appointment."

Gus put one leg on the floor and raised from the stool. He extended his hand and said loud enough for any listening ears, "I'm glad I ran into to you, Nick. See you again sometime."

They shook hands and Nick left, striding purposely through the bar with his nose up, looking from side to side.

Seated back on the stool, Gus returned to his martini and watched the peacock with a wry smile. Nick was a jerk just like the kid. He didn't envy their coaching staff if Mike decided on their school. Four years of plenty of headaches would be ahead for them. But headaches that could bring a national championship. He smiled to himself and turned to look out at the river where a freighter was passing by the raised Michigan Avenue

Bridge on its way to the Mississippi. Gus had paid his dues as a coach in college and also in the pros. The pay was peanuts. He mused to himself sardonically that back when he coached professors were making more than a football coach. But now was his chance to build a nest egg, which would well happen if they landed Bonjanovich.

The freighter was through the bridge and he could see the faces of the seamen leaning against the ship's railing. Tanned and healthy looking, they casually gazed over the sights of the big city. In a couple of days he suspected that they would be in New Orleans. He loved the Quarter. Not a bad place to settle in with a nest egg he thought as he signaled the bartender for another martini.

CHAPTER 8

A ndrew Sikorski lived with his father in a brick bungalow on a quiet street with extended lawns in Oak Park.
Tom Sikorski was once part of an elite team of scientists
that had created the Bomb in Los Alamos, New Mexico. Being a
member of this discretely celebrated group that shortened the
war and changed the world forever, Sikorski's and his family's
future seemed bright. But, unfortunately, that was not to be. His
wife, a Polish émigré, died tragically by her own hand, and then
Tom's adopted son left home due to a bitter disagreement
between the two. And during this nearly unbearable period,
Tom was faced with an appalling dilemma at work. His boss, a
valued friend and Tom's mentor, was the subject of a political
witch-hunt, and Tom was asked to betray him. Tom recognized
that the man was being falsely accused, and he refused to let
him down. This cost Tom his job and a promising career.

After the death of his wife and his termination from the Lab,
Tom moved with Andrew to Chicago to join the faculty of the
Physics Department at the Illinois Institute of Technology. Oak
Park was a relatively easy commute by elevated train to the
school in Chicago, and the western suburb provided a better
environment than did the city for Andrew's rearing.

Tom was reading and smoking a pipe in the downstairs
study when Andrew came in from school. He looked up and
took the pipe from his mouth.

"How was your first day?"

Andrew dropped his book bag at his feet and shook his

head. "Can I go to another school?"

Tom was perplexed at the unexpected statement by Andrew for Malloy had a superb science program, plus the school was purportedly well run by the priests.

"What happened, son?" Tom asked.

Andrew answered bleakly, "It's just not what I had presumed it would be."

"Did you have trouble with any students?"

"Not really," Andrew replied.

His father waited, unable to imagine his son having any sort of disagreement with another boy.

"Maybe I'm making too much of things," Andrew finally said. "I need to give the school a chance."

Tom nodded watchfully. "One day doesn't tell much."

"That's true," Andrew said with a forced laugh. He picked up his book bag and went up the stairway to his room.

Tom leaned back in his chair. He worried considerably about Andrew in other ways. Though the boy had a good head on his shoulders and was never any trouble, Tom realized that the death of his mother and then the departure of his adopted brother had affected the boy deeply. He talked to Andrew about seeing a doctor, but the boy would have none of it. He said that he would sort things out himself. Tom reluctantly gave in. Andrew was a brilliant and an astute boy, and his father felt that he should be able to work these problems out himself. But it was quite a load for anyone, and it bothered his father. Tom put a match to his pipe to get it going again, and puffed on it thoughtfully looking up the stairway that his son had just climbed.

CHAPTER 9

Located several miles into the city east from Oak Park was the home of Tony Barbini. Tony's father was in the den reading the afternoon paper with a freshly lit cigar between his fingers when his son arrived decidedly late on his first day of high school. On a lamp table to his left was the manhattan his wife dutifully prepared each night before dinner. Jack Barbini had big shoulders and a strong face with a receding hairline. Tony came in through the back door between the den and the kitchen where his mother had the ironing board up.

"Your dinner's on the stove, kiddo, cold as usual," Eileen Brennan Barbini said through a bobbing cigarette as she pounded an old iron on a shirt collar. She was plump with blue eyes and dark hair.

"And it will be delicious as always, Eileen Brennan," Tony patronized her, hustling around the board to kiss her on the cheek.

She took the cigarette from her mouth and held it to the side.

"Don't be calling me that, young man. You'd better show your mother some respect."

He kissed her again and said, "What's for dinner."

"What's it matter. It can't taste good, being so late that you are."

"My favorite stew!" He picked up a spoon from the stove and tried a sample.

"It needs to be heated back up first," his mother chided slapping at his hand.

Tony dropped the spoon and went into the den to join his father and his sister, Mary Margaret. Jack Barbini looked over his paper. He drew on the cigar and sent a slow stream of blue smoke toward the ceiling. Next to him his daughter was making her normal commotion from her special chair.

"And how was your first day in higher education?" the elder Barbini asked his son.

"It was an outstanding first day, Dad," he answered going over to his sister. As he neared, her excitement grew and her steel constraints clanged with the quaking of her pathetic body. Tony squatted down on his haunches so that he was looking up at his sister.

"How was your day, Mary?"

Her chair rattled louder. Due to a mishap at birth Tony's older sister possessed a perfectly normal mind that was trapped in a wrecked body. She adored Tony and Tony adored her immensely.

"You should've seen my first day at school, Mary Margaret. It's a big building with lots of people running all over the place. And everybody liked your brother. The teachers, the priests, the students and even those dumb old football players."

She shook wildly and mouthed guttural sounds.

"And I met a new friend. His name is Andy and he's as smart as a whip. I'll bring him over. You'll like him. Maybe this Friday when there's a sock hop at school. He's not the dancing type, but I'll get him to go."

Mary Margaret was beside herself, then she tired down and Tony got up. He brushed his finger affectionately across her cheek and took a wash rag from a table to wipe spittle from her face.

After another stream of blue smoke, Jack Barbini said to his son, "I noticed your books in your room, all neatly stacked on your bed while you were in school. Last I heard you still have to be a student at Malloy to go to its dances."

"It was the first day. I didn't need them."

"Really," the police captain replied. "You just sat all day in each class in a trance?"

Eileen Barbini appeared at the door wiping her hands on an apron.

"The dinner's ready. It'll be rock hard if I have to reheat it again."

Tony winked at his sister and started back to the kitchen. His father folded the paper and picked up his drink.

"You better step aside, Mom," the boy warned. "I'm starved and you might get trampled."

"I'm sure it's the same enthusiasm you had over at Malloy," his father mocked.

"Tony's going to do just fine, aren't you?" his mother encouraged him.

"I'll be the valedictorian," he said as he kissed her cheek on the way by.

CHAPTER 10

Friday came and both Tony and Andrew were still students at Malloy. That evening was the school's Welcome Back Sock Hop and Tony had been badgering Andrew to join him at the dance. Andrew would have rather taken a beating than go, but it was easier to agree with Tony and he finally relented. Tony, however, believed rightly that Andrew was just patronizing him, and much to Andrew's dismay, Tony insisted that he meet his friend at his Oak Park home.

"That's silly," Andrew said. "It'll take you an hour out of your way."

"I've got nothing but time, Andy. Besides, I haven't been out to Oak Park in a long time. It'll be good to see suburbia again."

Grudgingly, Andrew gave him the bus routes to his house in Oak Park.

True to his word, Tony arrived in Oak Park on schedule. He always felt he had entered a different sort of world when he went to many of Chicago's suburbs. Streets were considerably wider than those of the city. Lawns stretched much further from the street to the homes, and the cars were newer models with fewer, if any, rust spots. And the people dressed better. The children weren't scruffy like many of those in the city.

Tony had no trouble finding Andrew's home in the dimming light of the early evening. It was a brick bungalow that set back from the street. A driveway alongside the house led back to a garage that bordered a modest back yard. Through the front window Tony saw a man with a light complexion and short straight hair reading a book under a lamp. From a pipe in his mouth, little puffs of smoke rose in lazy intervals. Tony rang the bell.

"I'm Tony Barbini," he said to the man who looked as Tony figured Andrew would look in twenty years. "I'm Andy's best friend from school." He extended hand which Andrew's father took with mild surprise.

"Please come in."

Tony did. He wore jeans with white socks and brown street shoes.

"Andrew," Mr. Sikorski called up the stairway of fine wood.

"Please have a seat, Tony."

He sat in a hard upholstered chair in the living room and Mr. Sikorski returned to his chair under the light and crossed his legs.

"So you're a classmate of Andrew's at Malloy?"

"Yes sir. As I mentioned, we're best friends. He's a lot smarter than me, but I'm helping him with the social stuff."

"Really," he said crooking his head with a smile. "Social stuff?"

"Yeah. You know, getting to meet a lot of people. We'll probably meet some girls tonight at the dance."

"Oh?"

"Right. But it won't be like official dates or anything like that. We're a little young, you know."

"Yes, I guess you boys are."

He puffed on his pipe as Tony looked over the room that held bookcases reaching from the floor to the ceiling.

"You guys sure must read a lot."

Mr. Sikorski glanced around.

"Yes, we do. Do you like to read, Tony?"

"You know I actually have a problem with that. I know reading's important, but I don't want to miss anything."

"You're missing a lot if you don't read."

"Yeah, I guess I have to work on that." He looked around the room again. "Andy says he has an older brother."

Tom Sikorski hesitated, and then replied, "Yes, Jerry lives out of the state." Andrew appeared at the top of the stairs and looked down at his father and Tony in the living room. Though he wasn't looking forward to the evening, he dressed smartly in slacks and a pressed white short sleeve shirt. His hair was combed perfectly with the straight part to a side. Dolefully, he started down the steps.

"There's Andrew now," his father said.

"Come on, Andy. We're going to be late," Tony said.

"Are you sure you boys don't want a ride? It's much faster than the bus."

"Oh no sir," Tony declined. "A lot of girls will be riding the bus to the dance. Maybe we can make some acquaintances before we even get there."

Andrew rolled his eyes.

"Well then, just give me a call when you're ready to leave and I'll pick you up. The Oak Park buses have an abbreviated schedule later in the evening."

"It's been a pleasure meeting you sir," Tony said, enthusiastically shaking his hand.

"You boys be careful," Tom Sikorski replied, not sure what to make of his son's self-proclaimed 'best friend'.

CHAPTER 11

That night the Malloy gymnasium bore no likeness to the gym the boys used throughout the week for PE classes. It had been transformed to an enchanting Midwest field at harvest time. Scores of hay bales had been strategically placed and stacked and at each end were two authentic Indian teepees. Sitting cross-legged with straight backs in front of each were students in Indian dress with long pipes tucked into the corners of their mouths. They sat stoically, looking out perhaps to the vast horizon. Only the parquet basketball floor was left uncovered to dance upon by students in their stocking feet.

"Look at that, Andy," Tony exclaimed excitedly indicating the gym as he took off his shoes to check them in at a counter.

Andrew reluctantly removed his shoes also and turned them in. He was uncomfortable on the cold floor without shoes on his feet. Then they crossed into a fall harvest of the previous century.

"This is great!" Tony marveled.

For the moment Andrew forgot how miserable he was with wonder of how the lighting had been devised to create the appearance of a brilliant sunset illuminating gold and orange straw positioned expertly behind and alongside the teepees. He would perhaps have a visit with whoever was responsible for the illumination.

Buddy Holly's 'At The Hop' started up loudly through the sound system and Tony yelled over it, "Let's find some girls to dance with."

"No!" Andrew called back.

"Why not? This is a dance."

"I can't dance!"

"It doesn't matter. I'll dance one and you watch me. It's easy"

Andrew shook his head.

With that Tony ventured out to the dance floor with a plan in mind, leaving Andrew alone for the moment. Andrew saw that Tony had no trouble finding girls to dance with. For three songs he danced with as many different partners. Fast dances and slow dances. Tony seemed to be having a fabulous time while Andrew was equally miserable. He had a notion to call his father to pick him up when Tony returned from the dance floor.

"Come on, I've found some girls for us."

"What are you talking about!" Andrew replied with alarm.

"We'll make friends and have a good time. I'm sure there's a smart one among them for you."

"No, Tony," he protested, but he was already being pulled across the floor. As much as Andrew didn't relish talking with girls, he abhorred making a scene so he let Tony have his way.

Three girls with skirts to their calves and white bobby socks were standing with their arms folded by a small stack of hay. To Andrew they all looked alike though one wore glasses.

"Girls, this is my good friend Andy," Tony promptly introduced Andrew and then ticked off the names of the girls: Mary, Carmela and Susan. Susan was the one with glasses. Mary and Carmela could have been sisters with dark beehive hairdos while Susan's hair was brown with short tight curls and bangs.

Andrew said nothing and didn't look any of them in the eye.

Mary and Carmela rolled their eyes at each other while Susan said, "Hello Andrew. Tony said you're a quite a dancer."

"No, I'm not!" he replied with astonishment, looking irritably at Tony.

"He is a little shy about it," Tony put in. "He doesn't want to show up the upperclassmen, especially the football players."

"Are there football players here?" Mary brightened up, quickly searching the floor.

"They're probably in training," Tony said, "but I've gotten to know some of the seniors already.

"Really," Carmela broke in. "Which ones?"

"The quarterback for one."

Andrew shook his head in dismay.

"You mean Mike Bonjanovich!" Mary squealed and jumped back with an open mouth. "My sister knows him."

"Yeah, that's him. He talked to us just the other day. Ain't that so, Andy?"

"If you say so," Andrew replied dryly.

Tony's stock had suddenly risen with Mary and Carmela and he sensed it. Mary was the closest, so he grabbed her hand.

"Time to dance," he directed and she readily followed him out to the floor.

It was expected that Andrew, being touted as a skilled dancer, would pick one of the remaining girls, but of course he didn't. He became stone silent with his arms folded. A minute into the song a freshman, who appeared to be even younger than Andrew, asked Carmela to dance and she declined. Ironically, the boy thought that the girls were with Andrew, and he gave Tony's classmate a look of admiration. Aware of the boy's regard, Andrew felt even more uncomfortable, and would have denied the connection but might again cause an unwanted scene. With a change of songs Tony brought Mary back and returned to the floor with Carmela. He repeated the process with Susan, all the while Andrew stood mute as if the girls weren't present.

"Why won't your friend dance?" Susan asked Tony as they two-stepped to the Platters' 'Twilight Time'.

"Well, to be quite honest, Andy wasn't crazy about dances, but I talked him unto coming."

"Why did you do that?" she asked with a cocked head.

"Andy's a smart guy, smarter than anyone I've ever known. But he doesn't need to study all the time. I'm the one who should be home studying."

Susan laughed and Tony liked the way she laughed. She wasn't as pretty as the other two girls, but there seemed to be more to her than the others.

"Tell you what," he encouraged. "I'll bet if you ask him, he'll get out here and dance."

"You think so?"

"Sure. I got him to come to the dance, and he said he wouldn't."

Susan left Tony on the floor and marched over to Andrew and said, "Let's dance."

"What?" he replied with distress.

"Come on, Andy, dance with me."

"I can't."

"Sure you can. I'll help you."

"Really, I can't."

"Come on," she coaxed pleasantly with a charming smile.

Quite reluctantly, he stepped forward and gave her his

hand. The other two girls who were standing well removed from Andrew looked strangely at their classmate while Tony, from the dance floor, observed her with admiration and clapped loudly.

Moments later Andrew was standing stiffly on the crowded floor and Bill Haley's 'Rock Around the Clock' started up.

"Give me your hands and leave your arms limp," she yelled over the loud music.

"It's too fast!"

"Don't worry. Just watch my feet."

Susan suddenly became light on her feet, jitterbugging on her toes in perfect rhythm. Andrew watched her feet closely.

"I'll slow down," she said, thoroughly enjoying the music with a flushed face.

She lessened the tempo, but remained in rhythm and Andrew made a bad stab at trying to follow her. He moved with the rigidity of an ironing board, and the two girls on the side giggled. Fortunately, Andrew's back was to them and the noise prevented him from hearing them. He continued and Susan undauntedly encouraged him with a gleaming smile. Mercifully for Andrew, the song ended and he hurried from the floor. He was embarrassed, though he felt a strange and disturbing sense of pleasure in what he had just tried.

"You did great!" Tony praised, clapping again, as they joined him by the haystacks.

"Not hardly," Andrew said patting his hair to assure it still had a perfect part, which it did.

Andrew persevered as he watched others and was relieved not to dance himself any further that evening. Toward the end of the sock hop Tony suggested that they stop for hamburgers at a hangout not far from the school. 'The grill was near the bus stop,' Tony reasoned. They would leave the dance early so that Andrew would easily be at home on time. Andrew actually found that he rather enjoyed the company of Susan, who had already decided to join them. But Mary and Carmella were reluctant until Tony made it clear that it was his treat and then they agreed also. But then Mary remembered that her older sister was driving and was obligated to see the girls home.

"Let's check with her," Tony suggested. "Maybe she'll want to join us too."

Though she had little interest in being with Tony and Andrew, the prospect of time at a Malloy hangout and a bought meal excited Mary. She hadn't seen her sister for a while and figured that she was in the lobby smoking or maybe making out with a boy.

"Let me find her," she said.

Mary's sister Catherine and her friend Tammy were juniors at Sacred Heart, the same school the three freshmen girls attended. Catherine and Tammy had no use for the younger girls, but the use of the family car was contingent upon seeing them to and from the dance. Normally they wouldn't be seen at a lowly sock hop, but Catherine had heard that some of the Malloy football players would be there and took a chance that one of them might be Mike Bonjanovich. She had idolized him for two years and now she was old enough to do more than just eye him from afar. During summer vacation she had heard that he spent time at the Foster Avenue beach, and she managed to make his acquaintance there one Saturday afternoon. When he told her to stop by one of the Malloy dances to see him, she immediately got a hold of Malloy's social schedule.

Mary spotted Tammy alone leaning on a wall near the school trophy case smoking a cigarette. "Where's my sister?"

Blowing a stream of smoke upward into a fog that had gathered near the ceiling, the older girl pointed toward a stairway leading down to the basement.

Mary went down the stairs. "Catherine?" she whispered timidly near the bottom of the dark stairway. There was no reply but she felt certain that someone was down further on the next landing. Her eyes adjusted some to the dark and she saw a silhouette of two people in an embrace. Against the wall was a girl seemingly enjoying gyrations at the waist from a large muscular boy.

"Catherine?" she again whispered.

"What!" the girl replied abruptly in a husky voice.

"It's time to go and some boys want to buy us hamburgers."

"We're going to meet at Sal's for pizza," Catherine said and then coyly added to the boy, "Isn't that right, Mike?"

"Sure, if you say so," Mike Bonjanovich answered giving her a good feel that caused her to gasp.

By then Mary's eyes had adjusted further and she could see everything. What she saw excited her.

"Can the boys go with?" Mary asked thinking that Tony might be all right to make out with.

"Sure, if they're paying," Catherine replied. "You sit with them," she added.

So it was decided that they would go to Sal's, a pizza joint on Belmont not far from where the girls lived. They crowded into the Buick that Catherine was driving to meet Bonjanovich, unbeknownst to the boys, at Sal's. It wasn't until they had driven a couple of miles that Andrew realized they were traveling further into the city and away from Oak Park.

"Where are we going?" he blurted out from behind Tony's shoulder in the back seat.

"There was a change in plans," Mary said from Andrew's side. "We're going to Sal's. It's not far."

"But we'll be late. I can't be late!" Andrew cried.

"Oh, brother," Mary said, rolling her eyes. "Everybody's late sometime. You can call from Sal's."

"I'm always late," Tony stated. Then to Andrew, he added, "Besides, you were late the first day of school and you're still alive."

One of the girls giggled in the darkness of the car.

When they entered the brightly-lit pizza joint, the older girls immediately relegated the freshmen to a booth in the back and took a front table for four.

Sal, the owner, spent little money on furnishings but made very good inexpensive pizzas. He and his sons depended on a lucrative take out business and had the restaurant mostly for kids who wanted a place to hang out. Sal worked in a white stained T-shirt. His hooded eyes were dark and quiet. In the kitchen, which opened to the restaurant by a call-through window, were his two sons. Both in their twenties, they were dark like their father, but taller.

Tony ordered two large pizzas for the five of them and looked at the girls for the first time under a good light. Mary and Carmella had attractive made-up faces while Susan had plain features and didn't use make-up. He liked her eyes better than those of the others.

"So do any of you play football?" Carmella asked.

Mary exclaimed an impertinent laugh, "They're not big

enough to play football, silly."

"We're intellectuals," Tony countered. "We would play, but we have to spend so much time studying."

"That's too bad," Mary said thinking that maybe Tony could be a football player after all. Then she added, "My sister knows Mike Bonjanovich. It's exciting."

"What kind of interests do you have?" Susan asked Andrew, changing the subject.

Tony replied quickly, "Andy's a genius with electronics."

"Really!" said Susan.

"I'm not a genius," Andrew stated looking around for a phone.

"Sure you are," Tony said taking out a package of cigarettes to offer to the girls.

Mary and Carmella each accepted one and Tony lit them and then his own. The girls puffed amateurishly, feeling an air of importance.

"What made you get interested in electronics?" Susan asked.

"My father is a scientist."

"Really?" she said. "Where does he work?"

Andrew looked down at his hands, regretting that he mentioned his father's previous occupation. "He's just teaching now. At IIT."

"My brother went there," she said excitedly. "I wonder if he took his class."

"I don't know," Andrew replied wishing to change the subject but not sure how.

"Why isn't he a scientist anymore?" Carmella giggled foolishly. "Did he make a Frankenstein monster or something?"

Mary laughed a puff of smoke up toward the ceiling. "Don't

be stupid, Carmella," she chided, causing the girl to glare. "Does he pour chemicals into those glass jars like we see when we pass the chemistry lab?"

Andrew suddenly hated being there. "No, he worked for the government in New Mexico," he found himself saying.

"Good grief, where's New Mexico?" Carmella said.

"We drove through New Mexico when I was seven," Mary put in. "Our fan belt broke and we about died it was so hot."

"You can have it then. I don't like hot weather," Carmella stated. "Except at the beach," she added.

The conversation was taxing to Andrew and he still had to call his father. Then to make matters worse, he spotted Mike Bonjanovich and one of his friends come through the front door to join the older girls. He half covered his face with his hand. He thought there might be a phone in the back and excused himself. His departure from the table appeared to be abrupt.

"You made him mad," Carmella said to Mary.

"I didn't say anything," Mary defended herself, and then added, "So what if he's mad."

"He's not mad," Tony said. "He's just worried about being late. He's not as carefree as us."

"We're not that carefree," Carmella objected abruptly, not sure what Tony meant by the comment.

"Sure you are," Mary quipped. "You've been grounded more than me and that's a lot."

"Oh That!" Carmella said. "Sure, we're carefree."

"Do you get grounded a lot, Tony?" Susan asked

"Ground has been my middle name. Tony "Ground" Barbini. That's me."

The girls laughed at his silly wit.

"But not now that I'm in high school. I'm a changed man."

They laughed again. Mary was beginning to think more of Tony as she reasoned he might become someone with his funny words. She had at first thought that Tony was a bore, but then thought he might become a popular boy at Malloy and one worth being around. Though she still felt his friend was a real drag. It was at that moment that she saw the two football players at her sister's table and squealed. Instantly, she forgot about Tony as a possible big shot and envied her sister. She was tempted to get their attention but decided against doing so as she didn't want the football players to think that she hung around with freshmen boys.

"The phone here doesn't work," Andrew said returning from the back. He slid back into the booth.

"I saw a pay phone outside," Susan offered.

"No, that's okay," he replied with his head down slightly.

"Don't you have to call your father?" Tony asked.

"I will later," he answered nodding toward the front.

Tony then noticed the senior players at the other table and realized why he didn't want to walk that way. He also tried to become obscure, but then Johnny Costello spotted him and nudged Bonjanovich.

"Oh boy," Tony said under his breath.

"Look who's here, Mike," Costello yelled from the front table. A couple of snorts of whiskey on the way over had really charged him up.

"Well, what do you know," Mike said once he recognized them. "The kid from the neighborhood and the smart ass."

At their table Catherine turned and saw whom they were talking about and wasn't pleased that Mike's attention was being diverted away from her. She had plans for the night.

"They're just freshmen with my stupid sister," she said.

Ignoring her, Mike pushed up from his seat and moved toward the freshmen with Costello following.

"Beat it," Mike said to Tony, standing above him.

The girls shifted to see that it was the famous quarterback who had spoken. At first, they assumed it was a joke and Carmella giggled which didn't help Mike's disposition.

"We just ordered pizzas," Tony answered quietly.

"It doesn't matter," Costello hollered. "Mike said to leave, so leave."

By now the stench of booze came over the table and it was obvious that the seniors had been drinking.

"Why don't you leave us alone? Tony said. "You're being rude to these girls." Mike gave a nasty smile and was about to pull Tony from the booth when a voice stopped him.

"It's time for you boys to leave," Sal said wiping his hands on his apron from just outside the swinging doors that led to the kitchen. He was a good foot shorter than Mike who leaned back to look the older man over.

"What?" Mike laughed and Costello did the same.

"What are you going to do, throw us out?" Johnny said bravely, figuring that the two of them would surely cause Sal to back down.

"Why don't you boys just leave quietly," Sal suggested calmly, his dark eyes unwavering.

Something in the man's manner caused Costello to hesitate, but the liquor gave him plenty of courage.

"We'll kick your ass, old man."

Sal shook his head tiredly, "Not tonight boys."

The two sons appeared from the kitchen and moved to the sides of their father. They were thin and might not have been a match for the strong athletes, but the long pizza knives in their hands made all the difference in the world.

"Let's see how tough you guys are without those," Costello challenged hollowly.

One of the sons smiled while the other kept a grim face. Neither laid down his knife. Costello waited to see what Mike's response would be. The famous quarterback stared long at the two young men realizing full well through his boozy fog the advantage that they had. He grunted and pointed a threatening finger at Tony and then backed off.

"Let's go," he ordered Costello. He turned and stormed from the restaurant swatting napkin holders on his way out, causing them to crash to the linoleum floor. Following him, Costello did the same to the salt and pepper shakers.

"Where are you going?" Catherine frantically cried as the players passed them. Mike threw her a finger from his side without looking at her.

Catherine stood abruptly with her mouth open as she watched them disappear through the door. She turned to the table where her sister sat and marched over to it and grabbed Mary by the wrist.

"We're leaving!"

Mary cried to Carmella, "Let's go." Susan didn't seem to be included so she sat there stunned. In a few seconds the three freshmen students were the only customers left in the now quiet restaurant.

No one said anything for several uneasy moments and then Tony leaned back. "I hope everyone's hungry. There's going to be a lot of pizza here for the three of us."

Susan looked at Tony, then Andrew who sighed and shook his head. She burst out laughing. Then Tony started to laugh. The two continued as Andrew shook his head in dismay until it was all too much. First a smile came to his face, then finally he commenced to laugh with them as Sal and his boys returned to the kitchen to tend to the pizzas.

CHAPTER 12

The line was busy when Andrew tried to call his father from the outside pay phone to let him know when they had gone and what had happened. But Susan was able to reach her dad and, after she explained the predicament, he readily agreed to take Andrew home to Oak Park.

When Mr. Callaghan pulled up to the Sikorski home in his sedan, Tom Sikorski was pacing on the front porch. Puffs of anxious pipe smoke trailed him as he moved. He stopped and looked out at the car and sagged when he saw Andrew step from it with Tony.

"Where have you been?" he said in a raspy voice.

"It's all my fault," Tony said.

Sikorski glanced at him briefly, and then looked back at his son.

"Why didn't you call? You've never done that."

He was as much perplexed as he was worried.

"The line was busy," Andrew replied with tears in his eyes.

"I tried the rectory at the school. They said the dance had been over for some time."

"I'm sorry," he murmured and ran by his father into the house.

Holding the pipe in his hand, Sikorski turned and watched his son run up the stairs to his room. After a several moments, he said to Tony, "You boys were all right?"

"Yes sir, we were. I should have let Andy call from the school like he wanted, but I thought he'd be able to from the pizza place. He tried, but it wasn't the best place to call from."

"Okay, Tony. Thank you for coming up to the house with him."

Tony nodded and extended his hand, which took Sikorski by surprise. He shook it and Tony returned to the car. Tony waved, as did a girl in the front seat and then Tom Sikorski went into the house. In his son's room, he found Andrew face down on his pillow crying. He slid a chair from a desk out and took it.

"What's wrong son?" he asked still scared, but baffled.

Andrew shook his head and said something that was muffled.

"Is it the school?"

Andrew didn't reply. His father patiently waited until his son turned over and wiped tears from his face.

"What really happened to mother?"

Sikorski was taken back by the sudden mention of the upsetting question. He looked down at the floor, then back at his son.

"Why would you ask about that now?"

"I always think about it, Dad. And then people seem to invariably ask about her. Whenever I start to have a good time, this always seems to come in the way."

Tom removed his eyeglasses and wiped them with a tissue from Andrew's desk.

"Oh, God," he said more to himself and then fell into thought for a long while.

"You were too young then to understand all of this," he finally said.

Andrew waited while his father seemed to be trying to decide what to say. Then he set his pipe down on an end table and sat on the bed. "You know that she came from Poland, of course. I found her over there just after the war started when I was sent in to Europe to identify scientists so that they could be taken to America before the Nazis found them. During this time I met your mother and we fell in love. I talked her into leaving Poland, but she was reluctant because of her family there. She did leave eventually, of course. Then after the war she found out that the Nazis had killed her entire family." Andrew gasped and his father waited for several moments.

"She was never the same after that. She was in a strange land here and isolated because of my work in New Mexico. And none of the other wives spoke Polish."

"But what about Jerry?" Andrew asked now sitting straight up at the head of the bed.

Tom Sikorski hooked his glasses back in place and blinked to adjust his eyes.

"Jerry wasn't her son, not ours for that matter. He wasn't your brother, but your cousin. He was her sister's boy and he adored your mother. His mother died in a bombing raid and his father was away fighting the Germans. When it came time for her to leave, he begged that he be taken along. So we included him. And then when your mother...." His voice left him momentarily... "Well, when she died, Jerry felt that he had to leave." He rubbed his nose and his eyes. "Jerry's a good boy, a fine young man now I'm sure. Maybe he just couldn't bear to be around with your mother gone."

Tears were now streaming down Andrew's cheeks.

"But why would mother do what she did after going through so much."

"I don't know son," his father sighed. "Maybe it was that she went through so much. And then when I had the trouble with the government, I think it was all more than she could take. She was just too fragile by then. "

Andrew had always been reluctant to inquire further on the subject, but the conversation about his mother encouraged him to press ahead.

"What happened with the government?"

His fathered nodded and sighed for the second time.

"I was asked to betray a man who had done nothing wrong. Lie about a great man who had a lot to do with saving this country."

"But if he hadn't done anything wrong, why would you get into so much trouble for not lying?"

Sikorski picked up his pipe and repacked it. "That's a very good question son", he answered after some thought. "The times were such that people were terribly afraid. Afraid of a lot of things. So much so that they could be easily manipulated. If you didn't agree with those in power, they could make life quite miserable for you."

"And you refused to lie?"

"Yes, that's correct."

Andrew seemed to understand but was still bothered.

"I remember that you were gone....before mother died. Were you in jail?"

"No son. They never put me in jail. I was sent away on work. They didn't want anyone around who disagreed with them."

"What happened to the person they wanted you to lie about?"

He looked at his pipe and set it aside for the second time.

"They found enough people to agree with them and he had

to leave in disgrace. It hurt him terribly."

"And then you lost your job?"

"Yes, I did."

Andrew wiped his face clear.

"Why are some people so bad?"

His father smiled sadly and said, "It's always been that way and I'm afraid that will never change. Fortunately, there are people who aren't like that. In time people became sensible about the matter."

"What about this man. Did it become better for him?"

"No. Unfortunately, when proof was made public that he was innocent of any wrong doing, he had already died, a broken man."

"I see," Andrew replied quietly.

It was quiet in the room for awhile and then his father rose from the chair and started to leave the room, and then said, "This Tony, he seems like a nice boy."

Andrew shrugged his shoulders. "He's okay I guess, but he's sort of crazy. I never know what to expect from him."

Sikorski studied his son and then said, "Get a good night sleep, son."

CHAPTER 13

Malloy opened its football season on a sultry Saturday night in Soldier Field against a formidable St. Ed's team. The crowd, considerably large for a high school game, but lost in the vast olympic-sized stadium, was teeming with excitement for the team predicted to take the city championship. Many eyes were on the great quarterback warming up on the sidelines. Though his passing motion was smooth and casual, the ball left his hand with a pace seldom seen at this level of play. Each throw produced a murmur from the crowd.

Among the crowd were the Costellos and Bonjanovichs, seated at mid-field about ten rows up. The two women sat a row below the men. Except for having sons who were teammates and who hung around together, the two families had little in common. Al Costello worked as a park attendant for the city while Nick Bonjanovich ran a restaurant supply business. Bonjanovich was broad at the shoulders and trim at the waist with dark good looks, while Costello was balding with poor teeth and a beer-belly. He was a blowhard and Nick was cunning and manipulative. Tina Costello was round like her husband and somewhat of a dolt. Connie Bonjanovich, on the other hand, was tall like Nick with good looks, but dark rings under her eyes added several years to her appearance. She chain-smoked and preferred to listen rather than talk.

"Look at Johnny out there," Costello bragged, jabbing Nick with his elbow. "He looks great out there, doesn't he?" Then he quickly added, "Next to Mikey, of course."

"Sure Al," Nick said paying little attention to Costello.

Bonjanovich lit a cigarette that he held between his teeth. He didn't offer Al one for his concentration was set on the field. Mike was now taking snaps from Johnny Costello to run through a few bootleg routines. His fakes were deft with smooth and powerful acceleration to his run-pass option. With such speed and power he would put overwhelming pressure on a hapless high school defensive back. Nick turned to look over his shoulder to the press box where the college scouts would be. He had met most of them and he was certain that he would see several more before the night was out. One might bump into him in the john or underneath the stands where there was a bit more privacy. He'd receive an envelop or two with a pat on the shoulder and a word for Mike.

"Hey Connie, ready for a sausage sandwich?" Costello offered leaning down to Nick's wife with his garlic breath.

She shook her head. "Maybe later, Al."

"I know Tina wants one. How about you, Nick?"

"Not now, Al."

"You two are going to waste away to nothing," he said and opened a cooler at his side that was loaded with food and beer.

From it he passed a large sandwich wrapped in foil to his wife and took one for himself. Then he opened a couple of beers with a can opener.

"Surely you want a beer?"

"Yeah, I'll have one of those," Nick answered.

He gave one to Nick and offered the other to Connie who refused it. Tina took it and he opened another for himself.

"Connie, this is good stuff you're passing up," Al said

causing Tina to giggle.

"I'll have one later," she half-smiled noticing that Nick was uneasy about something.

He was indeed as he watched the new backfield coach standing down on the field rigid with arms folded. He was behind the offense as it ran through plays. Nick knew that Mike had no use for him and it bothered him that the little fruitcake was even on the field. He puffed anxiously on his cigarette until Connie reached for it to light hers. Unconsciously, he took out another one and lit it. O'Brien had assured him that this Cameron guy wouldn't do any harm, but Nick felt that his presence alone on the field was damage enough. He didn't like it. He didn't like it at all.

"Mike sure looks good, doesn't he Connie?" Al said, patronizing her.

Connie blew a steady stream of smoke to the side and smiled back at Al.

A few minutes later the game was under way and it began well for Malloy. The kickoff was returned to mid-field and Bonjanovich quickly moved the offense in for a score.

"Three plays!" Al giddily bounced on his seat. "Three plays and a touchdown. Did you see that line block! That calls for a beer." He jerked a can open and it foamed down to the concrete with a spray that caught all of them.

"Sorry about the bath," he rejoiced and his wife giggled. "Who wants another?"

No one did and the attention returned to the field as the teams lined up for the try after. Al shrugged and started in on what was left in the can.

"Come on, Johnny. Block!" he yelled loudly and Tina joined

him in encouraging their son.

The next two possessions also proved to be successful for Malloy as the team put as many touchdowns on the board.

"We'll score a hundred," Al boasted in a loud voice. His beer consummation was keeping up with the Malloy scores.

A couple of priests seated nearby turned their attention to Al.

"My son's out there," he bragged realizing their attention and the fathers nodded and turned back.

As the half was winding down, St. Ed had the ball deep in its own territory while the Malloy offense was on the sideline taking time to discuss its first half play. Nick Bonjanovich watched the group closely as the new backfield coach seemed to be ranting about something. He decided to move down closer to the field so that he could better hear the conversations.

"Use your brain, Michael," Walter Cameron chided, pointing his index finger at his head for emphasis. "They're keying on you on the option. You're making good yardage, but if you'd pitch the ball, we'd score every time." He imitated a pitch out in a not very athletic manner.

Mike stood with his back to the crowd and his hands on his hips. Standing nearby with their attention momentarily off the field and on the backfield coach, were Frank O'Brien and Jack Stone. From the stands one might think that a meaningful review session was in progress rather the makings of a lit powder keg. Bonjanovich was furious. In the classroom he would tolerate this little imbecile for he had no use for schoolwork. But on the field he wouldn't put up with his nonsense. This was his element and he was a master of it and his adrenaline was running high. He decided this would end here and now.

Through clenched teeth Mike said, "Listen you little cocksucker, don't you ever tell me what to do on the field!" Cameron's mouth dropped and he stood speechless. He waited for the quarterback to say something further, maybe to quickly apologize as they were in the heat of a game. But Mike only spit on the ground in disgust before turning to walk away.

Stone and O'Brien had both witnessed the vulgar display and Cameron turned to them for support.

"Did you hear that?" he cried in disbelief. "Did you hear what a student said to me?"

O'Brien looked intently at him for several moments then turned away to return to the game. Cameron was astonished that the head coach would say nothing.

"What about you?" he beckoned Stone.

"Walter, this isn't the time or place," Stone replied firmly, but with some sympathy.

"Well there certainly will be a time and place then," he stammered. "Father John will hear about this. I'll have a report on his desk Monday morning." Without another word and close to tears, the English teacher left the field to the stands and took two stairs at a time toward an exit tunnel.

The line coach watched Walter Cameron from behind knowing full well that he had no business coaching football, but, at the same time, the abuse from Bonjanovich was reprehensible. Even more inexcusable was his head coach seeming to allow the incident to pass. But Stone was a highly disciplined individual and he realized that he must turn his entire attention back to the game, and he began to do so. But the incident was disruptive and he found it hard to fully concentrate on the game as he had before.

CHAPTER 14

Sounds of jubilant celebration could be heard from inside the Malloy locker room after the game. But outside, Nick Bonjanovich didn't express the same joy as he nervously smoked a cigarette on the concrete ramp of the tunnel that led out underneath the stands. He was waiting for Father John Sobykevich to leave the locker room after giving a blessing to the team. Inside the room suddenly became quiet for several moments as the principal was likely giving thanks to the Lord. Then a loud cheer followed. A couple of minutes later the Malloy principal came out and was immediately approached by Bonjanovich.

"Father, could I have a word with you?" he asked discretely touching the priest's arm.

"Yes, Nick. What can I do for you?" he answered glancing down at Nick's hand on his arm.

Nick dropped his hand and moved with the priest further up the ramp out of earshot of those gathering by the door.

"The teacher was a mistake, Father."

Knowing precisely what he meant, the principal shook his head. "I had no choice. There was little time and no other qualified coaches available."

"But this is a championship team, Father. It's no time to have such a…" He stopped short of using his normal vulgarity and instead said, "Somebody who'll do more harm than good out there."

"What would you suggest I do, Nick?"

"Get Tom Baker back. He hasn't been convicted of anything. What if nothing comes of it? We're liable to lose the championship just because he had to wait to find out he's innocent."

"That's not possible. The charges are much too serious. I won't allow Mr. Baker to work with our students while he's waiting for his trial."

"Let O'Brien take over the backs then," Bonjanovich said in a raised voice, causing a number of heads down the ramp to turn.

"Nick," he answered firmly, "we've talked enough about personnel issues tonight. Why don't we just enjoy the victory for now?"

He turned to leave but Nick put a hand back on his arm. The principal looked down at the man's hand with resolve this time and then back up at his face. He said nothing but his eyes told Bonjanovich that he best let go quickly and he did.

Unfazed, Nick replied in parting, "Something's got to be done."

The principal at that instant longed for the gratifying solitude of his previous assignment in Church theology as he watched the man return to the crowd by the locker room door. He hadn't particularly paid much attention to sports, but as principal he had become an interested fan. He wondered now where this all would take him and the school. As he started up the ramp, a resounding cheer came up from the parents and well-wishers as the first Malloy player appeared from the locker room door.

CHAPTER 15

A few weeks later on a blustery Saturday afternoon, Andrew was walking up an alley near his home in Oak Park. On his way to the library, he was actually in Chicago as the border between the two cities jutted down the middles of various streets. Before he reached the library, he would be in and out of Chicago twice more. At that moment he was in Chicago with his father's old tan leather satchel, heavy with textbooks. Deep in concentration about the history assignment he would be working on, he barely noticed the rock as it whizzed close to his head. It was the thunderous gong when it struck an old oil drum used as a garbage can that so startled him. He froze and then heard someone laughing in a prairie to his left. He didn't at first recognize the boy, but then he made out a Malloy letter jacket and saw the familiar quarterback next to him. Mike Bonjanovich cocked his arm to hurl another rock and Andrew took off running. With an earsplitting bang the rock careened off a metal garage door where he had been standing and Johnny Costello laughed even harder. Andrew's shoulder hurt from the weight of the bag as he ran. A couple more rocks landed nearby before he reached a safe distance from the senior athletes.

Andrew decided to skirt the side street that he would normally take to the library as it would put him back in range of the boys. He instead continued up the alley that would add several more blocks to his route. To be sure that they weren't following him, he turned back and was relieved to see that they were now flinging what looked like asphalt shingles at the wall of a building to the south.

They were indeed sailing roofing shingles at the brick wall on the south end of the prairie.

"Did you see that little shit run?" Bonjanovich bragged.

"You should have hit him, Mike," Johnny Costello said as he let a smoldering piece of asphalt fly toward the wall. The shingles had been part of a waste pile in the prairie likely set afire earlier in the day. "Not that you couldn't have hit him," Johnny quickly added.

"You don't think I couldn't have hit him?"

"Of course you could. Look what you did in practice today. Every pass was on target. Every single pass was completed. Who else could do that?"

Johnny became nervous when Mike turned his nasty disposition on him.

"I'm the one that can't hit anything. That's why I'm a center," he grinned, hoping that he could change Mike's mood. He was pleased when the quarterback chuckled.

"Let's see if you can hit that fort," Mike challenged.

Johnny saw the wood structure, made of oil-slicked construction forms, up against a far side of the wall. He looked for a nice round rock and found one.

"Not with a rock," Mike said. "That's too easy. Hit it with one of those shingles."

Johnny dropped the stone and tried with several smoldering roof shingles, but he was off the mark badly with each one.

"Jesus, you're terrible," Mike reproved and picked up a shingle with glowing embers on one corner.

He sailed it perfectly at the wood fort and it settled above the structure before falling straight down into its midst. From inside the fort came a cry of protest.

"Hey, someone's in there," Johnny yelled. "How about if I fling some rocks at him?"

Before Mike was able to answer, a flash shot up from inside the fort. A moment later the entire structure went up like a dry Christmas tree with flames shooting toward the overcast sky.

"Jesus!" Johnny yelled and stood frozen with his mouth open.

Bonjanovich was also stunned at the ferocity of the sudden blaze. Then the awful screams were heard.

"We've got to do something!" Johnny cried and started for the burning fort, but was stopped by Mike's strong hand.

"They're goners. The only thing we can do it get the hell out of here," he said looking around to see if anyone was watching. No one was in sight.

"But listen to them," Johnny said in terror.

"We've got a game tomorrow. Let's get out of here or we might not be playing in it."

"But...."

But he was already being pulled away by Mike and, moments later, they were at a full run across the prairie and into the mouth of the alley that Andrew had earlier entered. Johnny stopped to look back once more, but Mike again pulled him along. They sprinted up the alley with Mike well ahead of the slower lineman. In the distance, the sirens of fire engines began to sound.

CHAPTER 16

"Terrible. It's just terrible," Thomas Sikorski said, shaking his head at the door of Andrew's room.

"What, Dad?" the boy asked from his desk chair, his mind still centered on his schoolwork.

"Three ten year old boys died in a fire this morning. One was the son of my barber."

Andrew let his book down.

"What happened?"

He shook his head again and said, "They were playing in a prairie over by Oak Park Boulevard and they were caught in a fire. I don't know much else."

A twinge of anxiety hit Andrew.

"What time this morning?" he asked in a weak voice.

His father looked strangely at him. Then he answered, "I'm not sure. Why, son?"

Andrew only closed his eyes and shook his head as a tear fell down his cheek. Thomas moved to him and pulled his son's head to his waist.

"Yes, it is an awful thing," he said gently to the boy, thinking that he was just being sensitive to the tragedy.

CHAPTER 17

Heads turned that Monday morning when Mike Bonjanovich took Andrew aside on a stair landing between classes. Fellow freshmen were impressed that one of their own was being noticed by the great quarterback while others just thought it strange.

"Where were you going Saturday?" Mike asked looking down at the anxious student. The senior had learned in the Tribune what he had expected; that the boys had perished in the fire and it was time to cover his trail.

"To the library," Andrew answered, avoiding the senior's dark callous eyes.

"Yeah, and what did you see?"

"I don't know what you mean," he stammered.

"It's simple kid. If someone asks you, did you see anything or anybody worth mentioning?"

He kept his eyes down. "No, not really."

The senior stared at the boy a long while and then finally smiled, "You're a smart kid. That's exactly what you tell someone if they ask you about it. You understand?"

Andrew nodded. The quarterback then left him standing on the stair landing and Andrew leaned back against the wall to support his shaking legs. The nagging fear that had kept him awake the past two nights was unfortunately well founded. He now realized that the two football players were surely involved somehow in the deaths of the boys in the prairie. Why was all of this happening to him he wondered as the bell rang for the next period? Dripping perspiration and light-headed, he pushed off from the wall and managed to start to his next class on very weak legs.

The strange meeting hadn't been lost on Father Sadak, who was standing nearby enjoying a cigarette between classes. He had observed the exchange and now watched the Sikorski boy walk past him in apparent grief. He wondered what a big shot like Bonjanovich would have to say to such a small fry. It was quite strange, he thought, for the star football player to take notice of the boy. From that first day, he had no use for Sikorski and the other freshman, that impudent Barbini. Father Principal had chastised him because of them. As insolent as the senior athlete was, maybe he would run these two off. Maybe they would transfer to a heathen public school and be out of his hair for good. He felt that it would be just and propitious for the Lord's school to have them gone. He took a last deep drag and exhaled upward, then stubbed the cigarette out in the palm of his hand so that he could enjoy the remainder of the butt later.

CHAPTER 18

That same morning Walter Cameron stopped by the coaches' office to confront the head football coach.

To the disappointment of Frank O'Brien, the English teacher had continued on as a coach after the outrageous verbal assault by Bonjanovich at Soldier Field. With the support of Father John, Cameron decided to carry on as the team's backfield coach, in name only of course. That weak sister of a principal, O'Brien fumed, had even raked him over the coals about the Bonjanovich incident, and then he was obliged to bring Mike in for a good talking to. O'Brien was afraid that the hot-tempered quarterback might blow up over the issue, but he was able to talk sense to his senior star. If Mike would stay clear of the teacher, O'Brien promised to keep a leash on Cameron and handle the backfield duties himself. There's no telling what this principal might do with another outburst from Mike, and O'Brien wasn't about to let this championship season go awry. Now he had this fruitcake to deal with in his office and his patience was on edge.

Leaning forward across from O'Brien with his hands on the desk, Cameron stated, "This has to stop, Frank."

O'Brien leaned back in his chair and formed a steeple with his fingers.

"Don't call me Frank."

Cameron pushed back from the desk and turned for support to Jack Stone, who was at the shared desk working on his practice schedule.

Stone shrugged his shoulders. "I call him Coach."

Cameron returned his attention to O'Brien.

The head coach snapped, "And keep your hands off my desk."

Cameron had started to set his hands down, then straightened up.

"All right, all right, none of that matters." He ran his fingers through his wavy rich reddish-brown hair. "What matters is what is happening on the field. What you're doing is wrong and detrimental to all of the Malloy students playing football. You're letting the players make fun of me. In fact, you're encouraging it. Mike started it and they follow his lead. It's wrong for students to be disrespectful toward a teacher or a coach. But it's even more deplorable that another teacher or coach would condone such activity."

"What exactly do you want me to do, Walter?" O'Brien asked with annoyance.

"You're the head coach. You need to discipline Mike. Maybe even remove him from the team if he's not repentant."

With his patience already on edge, O'Brien chuckled disgustingly then leaned forward and said, "Listen Cameron, if you disappeared from the face of the earth, I wouldn't be greatly bothered by it. The smartest thing you did was to leave the field at the St. Ed game. But then you came back. The principal forced you on me and, instead of helping, you've been nothing but a royal pain in the ass. You think you're a coach, but you're pathetic out there. If I were Mike, I'd probably do the same thing. For some reason, I have to keep you. Now you can keep up this silly charade or you can do everybody a favor and get lost or..."

The head coach hesitated, then continued, "….or maybe I'll start telling people about you."

"And what does that mean?" Cameron said apprehensively to O'Brien and then looked at Stone who turned away.

O'Brien responded with measured words, "What it means, Walter, is that I know all about the type of life you lead. Malloy doesn't need any queers teaching its boys. Even your great protector, Father John, might have a problem with that."

Silence hung over the office. Sounds of basketballs bouncing in the gym became prominent.

"That's ridiculous. What makes you think that?" the teacher finally said with a distinct edge of apprehension in his voice.

O'Brien smiled but said nothing. Until that instant, he had only his suspicions, but now he realized he had struck home. He said nothing and continued to smile at the English teacher.

After several moments Cameron said, "Okay, you can have what you want. I won't coach any more."

He started to leave the office, then turned and added, "Frank, you're a terrible person." He just looked blankly at Jack and then left.

"Hallelujah!" O'Brien cried with his hands in the air.

At the other desk Stone found himself relieved that Cameron would no longer be such a distraction on the field, but he didn't feel good at all. Not at all.

CHAPTER 19

"What's wrong, Andy?" Tony asked that afternoon at a lunch table.

"Nothing."

"What do you mean nothing? Your eyes are red and you're not eating your lunch. Of course something's wrong. What is it?"

"Please leave me alone," he begged, sliding away from his friend.

Tony moved along with him on the bench and took hold of his arm.

"Come on, Andy. You know you're going to tell me."

Andrew pulled his arm away and emphatically stated, "No!"

It was the quick movement that caught the corner of Brother Vladimir's eye from the other side of the cafeteria. He was particularly alert this day for some of the seniors had become rowdy over the victory by the football team the day before. The rule violation had been quickly repressed, but it left him anxious. Swiftly he moved toward the present commotion, bringing the room to silence with fear and anticipation.

When he reached the table of the two freshmen, it seemed that only they were not aware of the brother hovering behind them. Vladimir saw that the two boys Father Sadak often spoke disparagingly of at the rectory dinner table were having words about something. On another day he might be at first amused that they were unaware of his presence, but not on this one.

"Can't you understand English?" he heard the blonde boy say.

Tony, facing Andrew with a leg on each side of the bench, responded, "Why the hell can't you tell me."

The brother's eyes widened at such profanity in the cafeteria of the Lord's school and he moved in. The first slap caught Tony solidly in the ear and, as the brother was about to deliver a second blow with his other palm, the boy, regrettably by instinct not seeing the brother, cried out, "What the fuck? You asshole!"

There was a collective gasp in the cafeteria with Vladimir's hand suspended above Tony. For a brief moment time stood still. Then the brother's upper lip flinched and his eyes narrowed as Tony turned to see immediately the grave blunder he had committed. Instantly, he brought his arms up to protect his face and the brother went nuts. It was mayhem. Vladimir pounded down savagely with one fist then the other as if they were machine pistons. He knocked the freshman down through the bench space, then pulled him back up, but Tony struggled, tearing his shirt away. This infuriated the brother even more. He held the boy at the biceps with a vice-grip and began to drag him toward the stairs leading up to the office, pounding him fiercely with his free hand as they thrashed about. In self-defense Tony swung wildly back at the brother, and in fact, caught him once on the forehead. The cafeteria turned to bedlam, but the brother's complete attention was on Tony. Students stood on their benches to get a better look of the carnage that was taking place after the pair stumbled past.

Upstairs, Vladimir dragged Tony to, and then hurled him into the principal's office where Father Sobykevich was in the mist of a conversation on his phone. He regarded the student on the floor with astonishment. Tony was bleeding from the mouth and nose and had a gash above his ear. The principal told the caller he would get back later and promptly hung up the phone.

"I want this boy expelled, Father!" the brother spit out, pointing down at Tony. "He is Satan's own servant! Right here in the Lord's home!" Vladimir paced madly in the small office dangerously close to Tony on the floor. He looked as if he might begin to kick him.

"Please Brother, calm down and explain what happened," the principal said and then buzzed Wanda to fetch the medical kit for the boy.

"He doesn't deserve to be helped," Vladimir protested, still pacing. "He fought me!" he added pointing again down at Tony. "In front of the students, he struck a man of the cloth." He snarled down at Tony, showing a mouth of missing teeth, "You might as well go right up to the altar and strike the Lord Jesus with an ax, you heathen imp."

He raised an open hand to strike the boy again but was stopped by Father John.

"Mr. Barbini, go see Wanda while I talk with Brother."

Tony pushed up from the floor and cupped his hand under his nose to catch the dripping blood that had already colored the beige rug. He stepped wide of the brother and left through the door to the main office. Then the principal beckoned his secretary to also call the boy's father at work to come to the school as soon as possible.

"Brother, now please sit down and tell me what happened," he coaxed Vladimir.

The short, brawny man of the cloth wiped perspiration from

his brow with a handkerchief, and then ran his fingers through his blonde flattop. He shook his head , smiling oddly.

"That boy is evil. Satan...." He didn't finish the thought but only shook his head vehemently, uttering strange sounds. The principal finally persuaded the brother to take a seat.

Twenty minutes later Captain Barbini appeared in the outer office where he found Tony on a chair in the waiting area. Wanda had at least shored up the bleeding from his nose. Working on a new cigar, Jack surveyed his son.

"Get into a fight with another student?" he asked.

Tony shook his head and slurred through a swollen lip, "One of the teachers."

The police captain cocked his head.

"A teacher did this?"

"Actually the cafeteria monitor."

His father raised his eyebrows and turned to Wanda. She busied herself in embarrassment with work on her desk.

"And who might that be?" he asked his son.

"Brother Vladimir. He's talking to the principal now."

"I'll tell Father you're here," Wanda offered loudly as she stood up and hurried toward the principal's office.

A moment later she announced from the doorway that Father would see them and stepped aside as the Barbinis entered the small office. Seated on a chair to the left against the wall was Brother Vladimir with a leg bouncing anxiously. The principal stood from behind his desk to greet the elder Barbini.

"I'm Father Sobykevich and this is Brother Vladimir," he said indicating the brother who smugly remained seated.

"Jack Barbini, Father," he replied, shaking hands with the principal.

"I'm sorry we have to meet under these circumstances and I appreciate you coming from work with such short notice, but this is a serious matter. Let's all sit down."

Tony took a chair to the right and his father sat between him and the brother.

"Brother," the principal asked, "please start by telling what happened in the cafeteria."

Vladimir showed his teeth. "This boy was in an argument with another boy, a bad boy, at the lunchroom table, using profanity. Horrible talk! A freshman using unclean words in our Lord's school! He should be sent away for that alone!" He looked at Tony and it seemed as if he might lunge at him, but he then continued, "Of course I put a stop to this abuse immediately and then this heathen boy turned first his filthy language and then his fists on me. He must be expelled at once! If he stays in this school a minute longer, he'll infect all of the fine boys of our school."

The principal turned to Tony, "These are serious charges Mr. Barbini. What do you have to say?"

"It's true," he managed to admit with thick words that were now hard to understand as he spoke through swollen lips. "I used language I shouldn't have. I was concerned about something that happened to my friend, Andy, and I was getting frustrated because he wouldn't tell me what was wrong."

"That's no excuse...!" Vladimir interrupted but was stopped by an open palm from the principal.

Tony continued, "Brother Vladimir surprised me and it hurt. It was just a reaction that I said what I did. I didn't mean it."

"What about striking a man of God, you little ingrate?" He leaned across Tony's father.

Tony was slow to answer. "I'm sorry Brother, but it was too much. You were hurting me bad. I had to try to stop you."

Vladimir began breathing heavily through his nose with snot forming. "See," he bellowed to the principal. "Look how he talks to me now. Even such punishment doesn't make a difference. Imagine how he will be as a senior. He'll have a gang of hooligans running the school. I demand that he be banished from school this very day!"

The principal leaned back in his chair and turned his attention to the boy's father. He pushed an ashtray closer to him for the cigar ash.

"Mr. Barbini, would you like to say anything?"

The captain tapped the ash into the tray and said, "Tony, leave us for a couple of minutes and close the door."

"What is this?" the brother demanded. "He needs to stay here to answer for his wicked sins."

But Tony gratefully got up and left, closing the door behind him, which did nothing good for the brother's humor.

"Why is that boy allowed to stay in our school even this long?" he cried.

Father John waited with curious patience as the captain puffed thoughtfully on the cigar and blew a stream of blue smoke toward the ceiling.

"Tony is far from perfect, Brother. He did wrong here and he'll be punished. I'll leave that to Father John. He seems like a fair person. But you, Brother, are a lunatic."

Already keyed up, Vladimir showed his teeth and started to nod vigorously.

"See!" he said to the principal. "See, what kind of a parent a boy like this has."

Such a statement was more than Father Sobykevich had been expecting from the police captain and he began to refute Barbini's accusation but was stopped by the Tony's father.

"Brother, I'm a police captain and I'm sorry to say that I know of you all too well from my work."

A perplexed look came over the brother's face, but he recovered quickly and said, "What sort of nonsense is this?"

Father John leaned forward with a sudden feeling of uneasiness.

"There's a private club on Broadway near Montrose. Upstairs are rooms where the members meet. Sometimes with each other and sometimes with younger boys. I'm sure you're familiar with the establishment and what takes place there."

"This is rubbish!" Vladimir said, pushing up from his chair.

"Sit down. I'm not through," he ordered and something in the captain's tone brought the brother back to his chair.

"You go by the name Peter. Saint Peter actually. Does that sound familiar?"

"Father, I have responsibilities," the brother protested, but the principal was listening to Barbini.

Jack continued, "Our hands have been tied so far by the Archdiocese. But no longer, Brother. I'll bring you up on charges myself if I have to."

The small office was abruptly silent as Vladimir narrowed his eyes so that one was nearly shut. Then he showed his sick smile.

"You're a bad man," he said pointing a finger at the police captain. "I know your kind. You'll do anything to protect that filthy boy of yours. You make up these outrageous lies." Then he turned to the principal with foamy spittle showing on his bottom lip. "This man and this boy must be removed from our school immediately! And I suggest that measures be taken to have them both excommunicated from the Church!" His head bobbed up and down and his right leg jumped nervously.

"Brother," the principal said quietly, "please go over to the rectory. I'll meet you there in a few minutes."

Vladimir seemed bewildered. "But what about my lunchroom obligations?" he asked with self-righteous anger.

"I'll take care of them for now."

Vladimir looked at the elder Barbini fiercely and showed his teeth again. Then he spun up from the chair and whisked from the office.

Both the police captain and Father John watched the spot where Vladimir had left the room for a few moments then the principal spoke tiredly, "This is true?"

"Yes. I'm afraid so, Father."

He shook his head and slumped back in the big leather chair and closed his eyes.

"I've always wondered about Brother. His idiosyncrasies have been made fun by all of us, but......."

Jack waited patiently to let the principal think things through.

"I will take care of him," Father John finally said.

"He should go to jail, but I know that will not be allowed to happen," Jack said. "I'll let it go as long as he's not around children or students."

"Yes, I agree. I will take care of that. And I'll work on an appropriate punishment for your son."

"Of course, Father."

Jack was about to get up, but he sensed that the principal

wanted to say more.

Father John shook his head and said, "Jack, I'm very worried about the Church these days."

"How so, Father?"

"We just don't have enough quality young men who are willing to accept the calling anymore."

"It is a problem, Father, and one of these days this sort of behavior will become public."

The principal sighed, "Yes, it will. Perhaps it should now, regardless of how it affects the Church."

"The Church isn't exclusive in its problems, Father."

He smiled. "Yes, I'm sure you see a lot in your work."

Jack stood up. "I've taken up enough of your day."

They shook hands and police captain departed by the same door as the brother had.

The principal remained alone in his office with his thoughts. He continued to worry about the future of the Church. His studies of its past made him aware of the vast failings of the clergy. He wondered how many young lives that Brother Vladimir had been allowed to twist and then he sank with the thought of how many more of the cloth might be committing the same sins as the Brother.

CHAPTER 20

Father John kept to his word and Brother Vladimir was mysteriously dispatched the next day to the Order's retreat center in California for 'special training'. His sudden departure caused a significant stir among the students of Malloy and Tony became somewhat of a *cause celebre* in their eyes. Not only had he survived intact from the brutal beating by the brother, but it was also curious that the incident might have prompted the departure of the feared Vladimir. Fellow freshmen placed him in high esteem while even some upperclassmen took particular notice of him when he passed with his bruised and swollen face, which served sort of as a metal-of-honor.

But Father John wasn't about to let Tony off easily for he had cursed openly and struck a member of the clergy. At six the next morning he was instructed to report in the boiler room to Emil Wujcik, the school janitor.

Wujcik was a big man with large hands, clear blue eyes and heavy feet. Having emigrated from Poland, he possessed an unusually jovial disposition for a death camp survivor. And he took great pride in keeping the school tidy and well washed.

"So, you're trouble maker I hear about?" Wujcik affably stated from behind his bench in a thick accent as he poured hot coffee into a plastic cup from a thermos. "Want coffee?"

Tony shook his head.

"Too bad. Coffee good in the morning. Get heart beat good so can work good."

"Okay, maybe I'll have some." He was, in fact, falling asleep on his feet.

"Good."

The janitor poured a second cup full and handed it to the boy.

"Do you have cream and sugar?"

"Cream, sugar? Ha! Cream, sugar cost money. Black better for you."

Tony took a sip and made a face. The janitor hooted.

"You get start today in showers. Today, tomorrow, next day. You keep big shots feet from itch."

"You want me to clean the shower rooms?"

" Yes. Clean, disinfect, sparkle. Good enough eat off so big shots mess again," he chuckled.

Wujcik got up with effort and motioned with a hand over his shoulder for Tony to follow him. They crossed the hall into the locker room. From behind Tony saw that the janitor shuffled with a stoop. He seemed much younger when he was seated.

The locker room floor was strewn with filthy athletic tape, bloodied gauze and dirt from football cleats. The football team was the last to use the room the night before.

"Big shots messy," the janitor said.

They stopped at the showers. The stalls were also littered with tape and gauze and paper towels. Drains were clogged and the shower floors were covered with a film of rank water with urine and green and yellow snot. Tony looked over the soiled clutter with dismay and held his nose.

"First drain, sweep, pick up," the janitor instructed, indicating a push broom against a wall. Next to it was a wet mop and pail and a can of industrial solution. Wujcik picked up the can and poured a portion of the lime-colored disinfectant into the pail.

"Now fill hot water. Will kill germs and smell. Then pour out. Fill water only. Mop chemical. Keep big shots from burning feet." He laughed loudly then handed the broom to Tony. "Start now. Work good. Finish soon."

"This is impossible," Tony said. "It's a quagmire!"

"Quagmire?" the janitor aped. "Good word, quagmire." He laughed and left Tony, saying to himself again outside the door, "Quagmire, is good."

Tony could hear Wujick laugh some more down the hall, and he looked with dismay at the miserable job ahead of him at this ungodly time of the morning.

CHAPTER 21

Jack Stone glanced from his open apartment window down onto Armitage Avenue. It was an Indian Summer night. The mosquitoes were long gone so there wasn't a need for a screen. Across Armitage several young professionals were outside a new bar boasting loudly of their great accomplishments in life. Occasional slurs could be easily heard about the surrounding neighborhood, which was in transition. Stone noticed a few local kids on his side of the street smoking cigarettes while eyeing the haughty lads across the way who had entered their neighborhood. They would gladly cross the street and give them a good going over if it weren't for the tough looking bouncers just inside the popular bar. This could indeed be a dangerous place at night Stone thought, but he knew he could handle himself if there was trouble. It would be nice, however, to be out in the suburbs or on Lake Shore Drive for that matter. At his meager salary, though, such a move was impossible. Stone could live with this for now, but he wanted more. And more he wouldn't get while an assistant coach at a Catholic high school in Chicago. He had played college ball and spent a couple of days at a pro camp before being cut. He missed that level of play and the finer benefits that came with the job. And he wouldn't have to live among gun fire and police sirens.

He went to the refrigerator for a beer and thought about Malloy's season and his future. A lot hinged on the success of this team and the highly visible Bonjanovich. The great quarterback attracted college coaches like honey brought bees. Coach O'Brien probably talked with two or three each day. Stone had no doubt that his coach was grooming himself for an attractive assistant's position with one of the colleges; possibly one of the Big Ten schools. Perhaps he could also break into the college ranks with a championship season, the line coach mused. Maybe a freshmen job in the Big Ten, or maybe a line coaching position at a smaller college. Yes, a lot was riding on the team. And Bonjanovich, though an absolute jerk, was the key to the championship. The competition in this league was intense and there was no question that the Malloy quarterback was the link to a championship. Jack leaned back on a sagging and frayed couch and took a drink from the beer can. He was a principled individual so he felt somewhat uncomfortable about the hypocrisy of letting the brash quarterback have his way on the field. He wondered if college ball, where money flowed freely, was like this; compromise with a capital C. At that moment the sound of breaking glass came from the street. Immediately following was the sound of people running. A minute later a police siren blared and tires squealed not far away. It was a typical night in his neighborhood. Stone drank some more beer and thought of life on a quiet college campus in a quiet wholesome town.

CHAPTER 22

Chicago police detectives Nick Fazio and Pat Sheehan surveyed the prairie in which the three boys had burnt to death a few weeks back. They were in the alley close to the spot where the rock had nearly caught Andrew's head that morning. Fazio, the shorter and stockier of the two, turned with his hands in his jacket pockets to look over the neighborhood. Sheehan, lean with reddish hair and blue eyes, stared at the scorched wall against which the fort had stood. It was the only sign left of the terrible tragedy. The charred wood had been quickly removed once the Oak Park police had completed its investigation. Technically, the prairie was in Chicago but the young boys all resided in Oak Park and the block was considered to be part of the suburb. Oak Park had immediately taken over the investigation and it didn't receive any major objections from the Chicago police as they generally had their hands full in the city. A burning shingle was determined to be the cause of the fire and the case was still open. Relatives of one of the boys lived in the Chicago Austin district, and enough noise was made to bring the Chicago cops into the picture.

"Had to be kids throwing the shingle onto the wood," Fazio said.

"The cops here think the boys might have been playing with it when the fort went up," Sheehan replied.

Fazio shook his head. "The pile of shingles was forty yards away. It's unlikely they would bring something like that into the fort."

"A long way for a kid to throw one of those."

"You ever sail a flattened popcorn box at a movie house?" Fazio asked and his partner smiled.

"The question is did a kid know the boys were in the fort and what did he do after the fire started?" Fazio said as he scanned the neighborhood again.

Sheehan joined him. "Lots of windows for people to see something."

"Let's get started," Fazio said.

Sheehan took the homes with back porches facing the alley while Fazio began with the buildings across the street to the north. For most of the day they questioned neighbors without much progress. About mid-afternoon as daylight was starting to wane, they met in front of an apartment building to the north of the prairie.

"I don't know Pat," the shorter one said, "we might want to move on to something else. It was probably an accident anyhow."

"Yeah, maybe. Here comes a lady. Let's see if she has anything to say."

Pulling a wire shopping cart toward them was a middle-aged woman with large frightened eyes. She wore a buttoned cloth coat with a babushka tied tight on her head. Sheehan approached her with his badge held up and the woman's eyes grew even larger.

"Detective Sheehan, ma'am. We'd like to ask you some questions."

She stared at the badge, then at Sheehan.

"This is Detective Fazio."

She looked at Fazio then back to Sheehan and said nothing.

"You might have heard about the boys caught in the fire over hear," Sheehan said indicating the prairie. Might you have seen anything suspicious that morning? Maybe somebody running?"

She shook her head vigorously then took her cart and hurried away.

"I'm sure down deep she trusts you," Fazio quipped.

Sheehan raised his brow and looked down at a basement window of the apartment building.

"Did you see that?"

"What?" Fazio replied following his partner's glance.

"A curtain moved there. Let's give it a try."

They went down the few steps and Sheehan rapped on the back door with his knuckles. "Police," he called out and knocked again.

The door opened to a chained safety latch and an old woman appeared through the space. Sheehan showed his badge.

"Can we come in ma'am? We'd like to see if you can help us about the fire across the street."

She contemplated a moment, then undid the chain and opened the door further. She stepped aside and detectives entered the basement apartment. She closed the door behind them and locked and chained it.

"Is there some place we can sit?" Fazio asked.

The lady shuffled past them and indicated with a hooked finger over her shoulder for them to follow. Fazio smiled to his partner and they followed her passing through a utility room across a concrete floor before coming into a living area. In one room she had all the essentials; a roll out couch, a refrigerator, a kitchen table with chairs, a radio on a shelf that also contained canned goods and cereal, and a small TV on a stand by a concrete wall. The detectives sat at the table and she took a seat on the edge of the couch.

"Would you boys like some tea?"

"No ma'am. We won't be long," Sheehan replied.

A toilet flushed upstairs and water ran along a waste pipe above them. Her eyes looked up at the pipe until the water passed and then said, "A terrible thing that fire. It was so sad about those poor boys."

"Do you remember seeing anyone in the prairie before the fire started?" Fazio asked leaning toward her.

She thought awhile and then said, "No, I don't think so."

"How about in the street or maybe outside your window?" Sheehan teamed from across the table.

She thought some more. The floor above her creaked from a person's steps. She didn't look up this time.

"Now I seem to recall that there were some boys in the alley. Two boys, I believe."

"Did you recognize them?" Fazio asked with interest.

"No, I don't think so. They were older boys."

"Do you remember what they were wearing," Sheehan asked. "Anything distinctive?"

"Distinctive," she considered to herself. "Why yes. One of the boys had a jacket with an initial on it." She pointed to her chest. "Right here."

"Do you recall which initial it was?" Fazio asked.

"Which initial? No, I don't think so. But it was like a jacket that little Tommy wears."

"Little Tommy?" Fazio questioned with a puzzled look.

"Yes, little Tommy Doyle from down the street. He goes to the high school here and has one of those jackets. It wasn't Tommy in the alley, of course. I would've recognized him."

"Of course," Sheehan agreed.

The two cops looked at each other and Sheehan spoke.

"Ma'am, would you mind if we brought you a few jackets to take a look at?"

"Why of course not. I've got all the time in the world."

The two men rose from the table.

"You've been very helpful," Fazio said.

"You sure you wouldn't like some tea?"

"Maybe next time," he smiled.

Outside the apartment Sheehan looked over the neighborhood again.

"Never thought that it might be an older kid."

"It's pretty thin," Fazio advised.

"But it's all we've got."

Fazio nodded. "I'll get a list of all the schools within five or six miles."

CHAPTER 23

With some reluctance Bill Callaghan agreed to let his daughter, Susan, go along with Tony to the Malloy Fall dance. The incident with Brother Vladimir had become notorious with both the students and their parents. In the eyes of many Tony was trouble and one to avoid. Callaghan had met and liked the boy, though the incident with the brother did leave him somewhat uncertain about Tony.

"He's okay, Dad," Susan laughed when he brought up the matter. "Kind of nutty at times, but a good guy."

"How about if I drive you two?"

"Dad, we can take the bus. That's the enchanting part."

"Enchanting? It's the same bus you take to school every day. How can a Chicago bus be enchanting?"

"But it's different at night going to a dance."

"Well, how about if I drive you to his house? I'm sure his parents would probably want to meet us. Maybe your mother will want to go."

"That would be fine, Dad," she said with a coy smile.

Callaghan winced at his daughter's growing maturity. Wasn't it just yesterday that her interests were in dolls and holding his hand at the zoo? Now she had all those hidden meanings, though innocent for now, in what she said. He was proud of his little girl, but she wasn't little any more. Callaghan checked and his wife opted not to accompany them to the Barbini's.

"We'll look like a tribe going over there to inspect them!"

Susan's mother stated emphatically. "Besides, I might miss Ed Sullivan."

By the time they reached the Barbini home Bill Callaghan was feeling remorseful that he didn't trust his daughter's judgment.

"You go ahead honey," he said pointing at Tony's front door.

"No, come on Dad," she urged from the passenger seat. "I want you to meet them."

"That's okay. I'll just make sure you get into the house," he smiled.

She kissed him on the cheek and squeezed his hand.

"Have a good time honey."

"We will. Thank you Dad."

Tony met her at the door and waved to her father as he pulled from the curb.

"Come on in and meet everyone."

In the kitchen she met Eileen Barbini working at the table on the evening crossword puzzle with a cigarette burning in an ashtray.

"Ah, an Irish lass. It's about time I got some support with all these Dagos around here."

Susan laughed and brushed her hair back from her brow.

"Come on," Tony directed and took her hand. "Let's go back and meet Dad and Mary Margaret."

Tony's sister at first was quiet when Susan stepped into the den with him. Jack Barbini put down his newspaper and stood up from his chair.

"Well hello," he said before Tony could introduce her.

"Hi Mr. Barbini. I'm Susan Callaghan," she offered with a

smile and moved a couple steps closer to shake his hand.

With that Mary Margaret came to life and shook her constraints. Susan went over to her and squatted in front of the chair.

"Hello Mary Margaret. Tony's told me a lot about you."

She rattled the chair wildly in glee and Susan put her hand on her arm and the girl's eyes rolled unevenly.

"She's happy," Tony said.

"I can see that," Susan agreed.

"See what happens when an Irish lass is in the house," Eileen said from the doorway.

Susan smiled. "I don't have a sister, Mary Margaret, but I have an older brother who's in college now."

The girl rocked from the attention, her long bony hands flapping hard against the chair.

Tony stood up. "We better get going. If we're late, Andy won't stay." To his parents he said, "We talked Andy into meeting us."

Susan rose also. "It's nice to meet all of you."

Jack Barbini nodded from the chair to which he had returned as he was lighting a fat cigar.

"Don't keep Tony out real late," his mother said blandly. "He's not used to it."

Susan chuckled and said good-by to Mary Margaret who responded nosily.

"You're family is wonderful, Tony," Susan said on the bus. Traffic was sparse and the bus rocked from side to side as the driver rambled along over the speed limit.

"You think so?" Barbini humored her.

"I'm serious. I liked them immediately."

"Yeah, they're okay." Then he asked, "How are your friends from school?"

"Mary and Carmella? I'm not sure. I don't think they're all that impressed with me."

"Well, that's dumb."

"They're not really friends. It was the first week of school you know. We girls can't go to a guy's dance alone."

"Why not? I'd go to your dance alone."

"It's not the same, silly."

"Yeah, maybe not."

They rode along in silence for a block holding on the seat back in front of them as the near empty bus with old shocks rocked and swayed as the driver raced to keep on schedule.

"You know something that's funny," Barbini said as the bus pulled back into traffic. "The janitor I help in the morning?"

" The guy from Poland you've talked about?"

"Yes."

"Everybody thinks he's dumb. The dumb DP they call him.

"That's terrible."

The Italians call him the dumb Polack. The Polish kids just call him a DP. That's for Displaced Person."

Susan shook her head in disgust.

"But you know," he continued, "he isn't dumb at all. He might sound dumb, but when I talk to him, he seems to always know what I'm thinking. Hell, I don't know what I'm thinking."

"He's in a different land. It's probably hard for him to communicate."

Barbini shook his head. "I think he enjoys that people think he's dumb. It's almost like he's playing games with them."

She thought about this awhile as the bus rocked. "I think I'd like to meet him sometime." Then she laughed.

"What's so funny?" Tony asked.

"I was thinking of Mary and Carmela. If I told them I'd like to meet a janitor, they would think I was insane."

Tony laughed with her and they enjoyed the rest of the ride.

It was a Sadie Hawkins dance. Malloy was renowned for its theme dances. In theory, the girls ask the boys to the dance, but at an all boy school this would be quite impractical. Tony suggested to Susan that Friday was the Hawkins dance and she might want to ask both him and Andy, which she did.

"My," Susan said gazing over the setting with wide eyes.

"It's something, isn't it?" Barbini said looking around the gym. Several members of the Social Committee were dressed up in Raggedy Ann costumes and dancing around the floor with arms flailing. The décor was not unlike the sock hop of the first week of school with bales of hay scattered throughout the gym.

Tony looked around with concern.

"I wonder where Andy is. He said he'd meet us out front."

"I don't know," Susan answered paying more attention to the surrounding. "This is charming."

"Come on, let's dance," Tony offered, giving up on his friend for the moment.

"I thought I was supposed to ask you to dance," she laughed.

"Well?"

"Well, then let's dance then."

They jumped out to the floor to dance to Chuck Berry's Maybellene and jitterbugged on their toes in rhythm among the students.

"It doesn't look like Andrew's coming," Susan yelled over the music awhile later as they stood by the soda stand.

At that moment Susan's classmate, Mary, approached with Carmella behind her.

"Hello Tony" she flirted. "Girl's choice. Would you like to dance?"

"Thanks Mary, but I promised Susan."

She gave Susan a flicker of contempt. "Maybe another time." She walked past the pair, as did Carmella who added a dirty look.

He smiled after they were gone.

"You've become a celebrity, Tony," Susan chided pushing her glasses back on her nose.

"You think so?"

"Yes, and I don't mind those two getting snooty because of it," she coyly smiled.

Tony gave her a playful tap with a finger to her cheek and then looked around. He had thought that Andrew would have made the dance.

CHAPTER 24

Andrew wouldn't be at the dance that evening nor would he be found anywhere else in the Chicago area for he was in South Bend, Indiana. Earlier in the day he had taken the elevated train to downtown Chicago where he caught a South Shore train to the northern Indiana city, the home of Notre Dame University. Andrew was there to see his adopted brother Jerry, for he needed advice and he knew of no one else to whom he could turn. It had been some time since he had seen Jerry and he had found out that he had taken a job as a typesetter for the school newspaper.

In South Bend the night air was cool and full of the pleasant smoky smell of burnt leaves. The commuter train had let him off in the middle of a downtown street and he then took a bus to the campus. Andrew couldn't have timed his arrival better for Jerry was coming out of the newspaper plant with another man as Andrew stepped down from the bus. Both men wore jackets with leather sleeves and carried lunch pails. Jerry was as Andrew remembered with broad shoulders, pudgy cheeks and narrow eyes. The two men were laughing about something.

"Jerry," Andrew called out.

Jerry immediately recognized him even though Andrew was a small boy when he had left New Mexico.

"Hello, Andrew," Jerry smiled and waved a goodbye to his companion. He walked toward his younger brother.

Andrew wasn't quite sure what to say, seeing Jerry for the first time in so many years.

"You long way from home little brother," Jerry quipped in his broken English with a broad smile. When he smiled, his eyes seemed to disappear into his cheeks. "You run away like me?" he laughed.

It was this wholesome laugh that Andrew remembered and cherished so. "No, not really," the boy answered. "I just came to see you."

Jerry looked at him thoughtfully and became serious. "Father not know you're here, right?"

Andrew shook his head. "I left a note, but I didn't say that I was going to see you."

"Yes. You come see me and no tell Father. Trouble, huh?"

"Yes, I'm afraid so."

Jerry nodded and said, "Yes, we talk, but now eat. Okay?"

With his anxiety Andrew hadn't thought about eating, but the mention of food caused him to realize that he was indeed quite hungry. They walked across the dark campus to a small café where Jerry ordered a cup of coffee for himself and a hamburger and fries for Andrew.

"You get big, no?" Jerry said looking Andrew up and down.

"I'm older, but not real big like you," Andrew answered uncomfortably.

Jerry nodded surmising his little brother's demeanor with a frown. "So, how Father?" Jerry asked.

"He's fine. I think he's happy teaching. Maybe not as happy as doing research before in New Mexico, but I can't remember that."

"New Mexico," Jerry mused. "Lot's room. Many mountains. Not much people."

Andrew hadn't come to Indiana to talk about those days, but

the opportunity was too great to pass. "Why did you leave?"

Jerry smiled and asked, "You come here ask that?"

"No," Andrew answered promptly. "I've got a problem, but I've always wondered."

"Bad time," Jerry said as he leaned back in his chair. "Nobody fault. It just time go."

"So much happened then," Andrew said. "When you left, I felt so alone."

Jerry smiled consolingly. "Yes, but I must go. No good stay then." He thought a few moments and added, "Andrew, Father good man. Just need go. Had go."

Andrew nodded and a minute later a waitress brought their orders. Andrew ate quietly while Jerry sipped his hot coffee. When the younger boy was through, Jerry asked, "So what big problem?"

Feeling a bit better with a full stomach, Andrew wiped his mouth with a paper napkin and began to tell the story that began on that tragic Saturday morning at the prairie. He left nothing out, including the threat by the dreadful Bonjanovich.

"You no tell Father?" Jerry asked after Andrew had finished.

"I'm afraid he would go to the police."

"Maybe police best," Jerry said.

"But I really didn't see them do anything. The fire must have started after I was gone."

"But you think they do it? And big one give you threat, right?"

Andrew nodded. "Yes."

"You in danger?"

Andrew hesitated, then answered, "Probably not if I don't say anything."

Jerry thought a few moments and said, "Hard live with now and later for sure. But you not speak now. You speak if asked. Then you be okay. Okay?"

Andrew knew that his problem had not really been solved. He wished it had just disappeared like the sun does at the end of the day. But he felt better having talked with Jerry. He smiled and nodded. "Okay."

"Good," Jerry said. "Now little Brother, we go my apartment and call Father. Then you sleep. Okay?"

Andrew nodded and they left the café.

CHAPTER 25

The next morning after a tour through the charming campus that was at its best with the fall colors on the leaves of the ivy-covered Gothic buildings, Andrew took a train back to Chicago at about the time Nick Fazio and Pat Sheehan were wrapping up their day at the Austin Precinct.

"What's going on tonight?" Fazio asked his partner from across a desk. The Precinct was in a rundown building with old metal furniture that made the Malloy coaches office seem upscale.

"I'm going to stop for spaghetti on Taylor Street," Sheehan answered. "Want to join me?"

"No, thanks. I think I'll catch a high school game tonight. Maybe have a few beers later."

Sheehan nodded. "Rush Street?"

"It's too noisy. I'll hang around the neighborhood."

Sheehan stretched. Where to next week?"

"Let's go back to Malloy."

"You see something there besides the coach being such an asshole about getting a letter jacket for us?"

"You're talking about Frank O'Brien. I've followed his team for a few years. He'll be coaching in college one of these days."

"Well, I'm not impressed." Sheehan continued, "Besides the old lady didn't pick out their letter jacket. In fact she seems uncertain about what was on the letter jacket, or even if it was a letter jacket. Another trip will be a waste of time."

"Maybe not. Remember she said the jacket was like one of

the kid's there? She might have been talking about Oak Park High School, and Malloy has the same colors as Oak Park."

The younger cop shrugged. "It's worth a shot, I guess. Did you get a list of the kids living in Oak Park?

"Yeah. There's several, including Mike Bonjanovich."

"So, who's he?"

"Christ, Pat, you really do need to follow football more. He's the best quarterback to come out of Chicago in twenty years."

Sheehan stood up to leave. "Is that why we're going back to Malloy? So you can meet one of your heroes?"

Fazio laughed, "Ten years from now we'll all be trying to get his autograph."

"With some of these guys it might take ten years for them to learn how to sign their name."

"Perhaps, Pat. But look at all the dough they'll make."

Sheehan smiled and shook his head. "Enjoy the game."

Fazio stood and watched his partner go down the precinct stairs. From a rack behind the desk he took his leather jacket and put it on for the chilly night ahead.

CHAPTER 26

At 9:00 a.m. on Monday morning Wanda Black dutifully set the two detectives up in a conference room next to the office. A fresh pot of coffee was on the long table with a plate of donuts she had picked up from the little store across the street from the school.

"Thank you, Wanda. This is very kind," Sheehan said with a warm smile.

She blushed and nodded with her eyes to the floor, and then hurried from the room.

Fazio reviewed the list. "We'll start out with the seniors. Get them out of the way first."

"Sure," Sheehan said reaching for a donut. "We get to see your hero first."

"You sure you don't want his autograph, Pat?"

"Don't think so, Nick. Let's get started."

The ever-efficient Wanda had a runner available to locate the students upon request, and each boy showed without delay. The morning went on drudgingly for the detectives. Some students clamed up, afraid that any past crimes, however trivial, might be uncovered. Others wouldn't shut up.

"Did you ever shoot your gun?' one sophomore asked. "Do you write anything on your bullets," another questioned. "I want to be a policeman or play for the Cubs," a brilliant junior stated before they had a chance to question him.

But none had any helpful knowledge of the fire. When Bonjanovich appeared later than his scheduled time, Fazio found himself embarrassed that he had spoken so highly of the quarterback to his partner. After five minutes with the arrogant senior, he privately vowed to root against Malloy in any game he might attend and he was glad to be rid of him.

When it was time for members of the freshman class to be interviewed, the interest of the detectives had waned considerably. Plus it was unlikely that any freshman might possess a letter jacket. They very nearly called off the interviews, but Wanda's keenness in her job kept them at it. She listed each class in alphabetical order, and by the time Andrew Sikorski was called, they were again ready to quit.

"What do you think?" Sheehan asked his partner, and Fazio shrugged his shoulders.

But when Andrew entered the room, the detectives livened up and sat forward in their chairs. This terrible burden had weighed so heavily on the boy that is eyes were red from crying and his normally neatly combed hair was mussed from his constant nervousness. Andrew was ready to get this terrible dilemma off his chest and in twenty minutes the detectives had a pretty clear picture of what had happened on that tragic morning in the prairie at the Chicago-Oak Park border.

Pat Sheehan put his hand on the boy's shoulder. "I know this has been hard for you, Andrew. But, believe me, it's best that you told someone about this."

He wiped the forming tears from his eyes and nodded. "Can I go now?"

"Yes, Andrew. You can go," Sheehan replied handing him a business card. "We'll be in touch, but call me or Detective Fazio if you need anything, all right?"

The boy took the card and left the room.

Sheehan stretched back in the chair with his hands clasped behind his head. "So the All-American boy was there, but said he wasn't."

"He's a pretty good liar," Fazio said.

"He fooled me." Sheehan agreed, looking over the list of students. "The kid mentioned Costello. He wasn't on the list. Should we bring him in alone?"

"Let's bring them both in," Fazio suggested. "Maybe work one against the other."

CHAPTER 27

Costello and Bonjanovich were dressing for practice when Wanda's runner found them. They were to report to the office conference room immediately, dressed as they were. Costello became quite nervous while Bonjanovich was visibly annoyed at his second summons. They left the locker room in football pants, T-shirts and only socks on their feet.

"What's this all about? We've got practice," the quarterback shot out angrily as the pair entered the conference room. In a T-shirt Bojanovich was impressive with the arms of a man.

"Sit down," Fazio said from his chair. "Some new information has surfaced that we want to talk to you about."

Costello took a chair quickly but the quarterback stared boldly at Fazio with his hands on a chair back. Then, he pulled the chair back and abruptly took a seat.

Sheehan leaned forward. Kid gloves were no longer being used.

"You two were seen in the prairie in Oak Park on the Saturday morning three boys burnt to death." He fixed his eyes on Costello who squirmed nervously.

"I wasn't in any prairie," he quickly replied.

"Where were you that morning?"

"I..." He fidgeted in his chair. "I can't remember what Saturday it was. I remember reading about it. It was long time ago. I can't remember."

"How about you, Bonjanovich?" Sheehan directed.

"I play football on weekends. I don't dick around in prairies," he stated coolly, looking directly into the detective's eyes.

The room was silent except for the sound a mimeograph machine that was turning out copies next door.

Fazio leaned forward with folded hands. "More than likely the fire was an accident. You boys tell us about it now and probably not much will happen. We find out later, it's gonna be rough."

He was talking to Costello who averted his eyes from Fazio's. The detectives waited. Bonjanovich was silent with contempt while Costello kept his eyes on the wall. "We didn't see any kids or any fire," Bonjanovich finally stated with boldness.

"Okay," Sheehan finally said. "We'll be talking with you boys later."

Costello wasn't sure what to do. When Bonjanovich pushed up from the table, Costello followed, leaving the room behind his quarterback on weak legs.

"You thinking the same as me?" Fazio asked his partner after the boys were gone.

"Yeah, they did it, "Sheehan answered slumping back in the chair. "They might even have done it on purpose."

CHAPTER 28

Andrew walked aimlessly through the halls, unsure as to what class period it was or where he was supposed to be. The policeman with red hair was wrong. He felt no better than before. After his visit with Jerry, he had realized that this path was the inevitable one to take, but he felt no relief. He wondered if this was how his father had felt after the security men in New Mexico had interrogated him. But his father said he hadn't told on anybody, whereas Andrew had. But then again he remembered that his father had only told the truth and gotten in trouble for it. Andrew had told the truth to the two policemen. What sort of trouble lay ahead for him? He wished his father had told the men what they wanted to hear and that they had stayed in New Mexico. He wished for a lot of things.

"Jesus Christ, Mike. We're in trouble," Costello whispered to his quarterback in the locker room even though they were alone.

"Bullshit!" Bonjanovich replied, slipping a custom made set of shoulder pads over his head. "Just keep your mouth shut. They haven't got any proof at all." He tightened its straps. "Okay?"

"Okay, Mike. If you say so."

"I say so."

At that moment Emil Wujcik turned into the locker room from the hallway. He was navigating a slop bucket by the wet mop in it. He smiled at the two football players.

"What do you want, you dumb Polack?" Bonjanovich snapped.

The janitor raised his eyebrows in mock fear. "Big shots!" He laughed heartily pushing the bucket back past them to begin work on the messy locker room. "Very important peoples!" he tailed off loudly, then laughed again.

"What a jagoff," the quarterback said as he slipped a practice jersey over his head. "Let's go. O'Brien's gonna be pissed that we're late."

CHAPTER 29

Later that night Mike Bonjanovich sat at the bar of a cocktail lounge on Mannheim Road near the airport. He was with Carol Fishetti, a hooker he had known for about a year. She was in her mid-twenties with dark hair to her shoulders. Her skin was clear and her brown eyes were large and round.

"A penny for your thoughts," she said bringing the martini she was nursing to her lips.

The quarterback was in a foul mood. He took a good swallow of straight scotch and shook his head. He was thinking about the meeting with the cops. He wasn't worried about them getting to him, but there were a couple of loose ends that did bother the quarterback. Johnny Costello might fall apart and then there was that punk freshman. He was sure it was the kid who had fingered them. Mike would deal with him later, along with that smart-ass friend of his. But for now he could use an alibi for that Saturday morning. He was running through a mental list of possibilities when a familiar face conveniently walked into the lounge.

Father Chester Sadak might be recognized as a priest in street clothes if one gave it some thought. He was wearing the customary black trousers and a black wind breaker. But instead of the usual clerical collar, he wore an open collar white shirt under a patterned blue and gold ski sweater. He sat at the bar near the door, a good distance from Bonanovich who was shielded from the priest's view by the girl. Sadak ordered a whiskey and lit up a cigarette. He blew a stream of smoke up above his head and nonchalantly looked over the dark room. On most Monday nights he ventured out to one of several cocktail lounges throughout the city. He always went alone and sat at the bar, seldom speaking to anyone. He usually stayed for two and sometimes three drinks, periodically glancing at his watch as if he was killing time before some sort of a meeting. Each of the lounges had one thing in common - women often sat at the bar. He had never approached any of these women and indeed had no intention to do so. What excited Sadak was the proximity of such a liaison. Just the realization of the potential of evil pleasure seemed to satisfy him. He went home to the rectory, content for that week. It was the fulfillment he required to get him through his tenuous days with the bothersome students at Malloy. He pulled long on his cigarette and blew another stream toward the ceiling. Then he enjoyed the first sip of the whiskey, feeling the delight of the heat passing down through his heavy chest.

"See that guy at the end of the bar?" Bonjanovich discreetly pointed out Sadak to the girl.

She turned back to look at Sadak and said to Mike, "He looks kind of simple."

"He is. Do me a favor and show him a good time. He'll probably take some coaxing. I'll pay for it."

She looked back at Sadak and studied him. "This'll cost you extra."

"Don't worry about it."

She said naughtily, "I should start charging you, Michael."

Bonjanovich winked and playfully patted her on the rear. "This is important. Do a good job."

"As always," she said smiling, and then gathered her small purse and cigarette case and moved down the bar. Bonjanovich picked up his drink and shifted to a table where the priest couldn't see him.

"Hi," she smiled, "Mind if I set here? It's my favorite chair."

"No, no. Go right ahead," Chester Sadak replied, scooting his barstool unnecessarily as if to make room.

The sudden presence of the attractive woman next to him seemed unreal. In all the Monday evenings out a woman had never approached him. Now a very attractive one was sitting down next to him when she had a choice of a dozen other chairs in which to sit. Secretly, he had fantasized meeting a woman as such, but had always cut off the thought so as not to sin greatly. But this is only a woman who had taken a chair next to him, her favorite chair she had said. He was making too much of it. He was confident that his sin could never worsen. He took a drag on his cigarette and blew the smoke up away from her and then kept his eyes on the liquor bottles against a mirror behind the bar. But in the mirror he could see her and she seemed to be meeting his eyes through the mirror. She'd taken out a long cigarette and he realized that she was waiting for a light.

"Do you need a light?" he asked offhandedly.

"Thank you."

He struck a match and she leaned toward him guiding his hand with a soft, noteworthy touch. Her eyes looked up at him from the corners as she exhaled through her nostrils while he continued the lighting. Her fingers moved from his hand which began to shake slightly. He quickly tried to disguise his nervousness by waving the match out.

Carol Fishetti blew a long stream to the side away from the

priest, and then said, "Come here often?"

"Oh, once in a while, I guess," he answered, attempting to appear casual.

"It's a nice place," the girl said. "I feel safe here."

"Oh, how come?" he asked, wondering why he had.

Joey keeps the rift-raft out. When I get lonely at the apartment, it's nice to have a place like this to go to. Don't you think?"

"Oh, sure. Joey. Is he the owner?"

"No. Joey's the manager. He doesn't put up with any nonsense. But that's good, don't you think?"

"Of course. There's too much rift-raft around."

The girl smiled, which made Sadak feel good. He thought he had put the statement in a humorous manner, but he wasn't sure.

After a few moments of silence, Sadak saw the girl had finished her drink and casually offered her another.

"Yes, thank you," she answered and signaled the bartender for a martini.

"Will you have another with me?" She asked eyeing his half-full glass.

He hesitated. "Of course." He waved at the bartender, as had she.

Sadak was used to a measured intake of alcohol. With more than one whiskey on the bar, he found himself rushing a little to catch up. His tongue and his inhibitions loosened considerably as the two made conversation and he was pleased to find her easy to talk to. Sadak was surprised to find that he was talking nostalgically of his youth in Chicago, and his days prior to entering the novitiate. He was careful not to mention his vocation. It wasn't important, he thought after all, that he mention his calling since he was out to relax and forget the day's rigors. The girl listened attentively, nodding and smiling when appropriate. She smoked as he went on, letting him light up new cigarettes. He began to get used to her touch on his hand and looked forward to it.

After nearly an hour she glanced at her watch. "Oh my. It's getting late."

"Yes, I suppose it is," the priest said looking at his watch with disappointment. He was clearly enjoying himself for the first time for as long as he could remember. But enough of this pleasure. He recognized that it was now time to return to the rectory.

"I'll have the bartender call me a cab."

"You didn't drive?" Sadak inquired with some surprise.

"No. Unfortunately I have to rely on others for transportation."

She started to signal the bartender, and then turned to Sadak as if the idea had just struck her. "Say, would it be too much trouble for you to drive me home? It's not far."

"Well..." he hesitated, feeling a tinge of panic.

"Cabs can be hard to get at this time of night," she said placing her hand harmlessly on his. "But if it's too much trouble, I understand."

"Oh, no. It's no trouble," he quickly stated, not moving his hand. Dropping a young lady off at her apartment didn't actually violate his vow of celibacy he joked to himself. The alcohol had made him giddy and was beginning to cause him to play silly little conversation games with himself.

"Thank you," she smiled and put her cigarette out.

CHAPTER 30

Her apartment was close by, just off of River Road. It was an expensive working apartment she leased by the month.

"Please walk me to the door," she requested. "The cab drivers always do that. It's scary at night."

Her request seemed reasonable and Sadak didn't doubt that it was a service the cab drivers provided. He walked her through the security door, past the lobby fountain and into the hallway of her apartment. It was a strange feeling to be walking a young woman through a plush apartment complex toward her room.

At her door, she placed an unlit cigarette between her lips before searching for her key. From what had become habit, Sadak felt that he should light it. She opened the door.

"Please come in," she said through the cigarette without looking at him. She went in and he followed, still thinking of the cigarette which needed to be lit. She closed the door behind him and leaned toward him with the cigarette. He lit it.

"Thank you. Let me fix you a drink for your trouble."

"Oh, I must be going," he said, not in full control of his voice. "Just one. You've been very good to me."

Not waiting for a reply she took her light coat off and moved toward the bar, which was well stocked with the best brands.

A night-light had been left on and she turned on a stained glass light over the bar, which added to the color of the expensively furnished apartment.

She brought the drinks back to Sadak and handed him a highball.

"Let me take your jacket."

"Oh, that's okay," he replied. But she had already set her drink down on the table and was helping him out of the black windbreaker.

"Let's sit down and relax."

He began to object, but she was moving him toward a couch with soft white upholstery. Sadak took a good drink of the whiskey and started to perspire. He had passed his limit some time ago.

Carol Fishetti leaned back on the couch while Sadak sat straight on the edge of his cushion.

"This is so pleasant just to relax, don't you think?" She said with her head nestled on the couch back.

"Oh, sure. I suppose it is." Sadak kept his eyes averted from the girl.

The darkened room was very quiet as the girl watched him for awhile. The sound of his breathing became more apparent. He stared straight ahead rotating the drink glass in his hand. She set her drink down and leaned forward, close to Sadak and gently nibbled at his ear with full lips and tongue.

"Don't," he said feebly, but he didn't stop her. She continued to gently kiss him about the head while caressing his body with her long practiced fingers. Sadak was suddenly breathing hard. He had let her take control. After a couple of minutes he began to involuntarily twist and squirm on the couch, unsure of what was now happening. Suddenly, he felt a great sensation and then an immense change.

"Oh my God!"

His dark pants were developing a large wet spot. Carol Fishetti smiled and kissed him lightly on the cheek.

"It's okay. I'll take care of it"

"What am I going to do?" he said with exasperation.

"Get out of your pants and give them to me."

"What!" he yelled.

"Come on. I'll help you."

She began to undo his trousers and he hurriedly helped her along, not sure what else he could do with the soiled pants. The pants were wide and they went easily over his shoes. His boxer shorts were a mess also, and she started to slip them off.

"Wait!"

"Come on," she directed and they were soon off.

She pushed up from the couch with the soiled trousers and shorts and said, "Take off you shoes. I'll be right back." She went into the bathroom with the clothes while Sadak remained on the couch, naked below his chubby waist except for his shoes and socks. He obeyed her directive and removed the shoes and then the socks.

A couple of minutes later she returned from the bathroom with a bowl of soapy water and a fresh cloth. She knelt alongside Sadak.

"What are you going to do?" he asked with alarm.

"I'm going to make you feel better."

He had no place to go without his pants and he didn't know what else to do. With a hand she nudged him back on the couch and then dipped the cloth into the water. She lifted his sweater and shirt slightly and, ever so gently, she began to clean him off. The water was warm with the fragrance of spring flowers. Sadak, at first rigid, sagged from the soothing movement of the damp cloth across his midsection. A small voice inside screamed for him to stop this nonsense, but it went ignored. For several minutes the room was quiet as she messaged the feeble priest. The pleasure was becoming too great. After a while something seemed to change and he opened his eyes. He could only see the top of her head. The cloth had been discarded and she had taken its place. He looked at her dark hair through the nearly closed slits of his eyes, then leaned his head back on couch. He was in an unreal place, in the hands of the Devil, but he had no urge to give it up. For some time this went on in the stillness of the room. Perspiration formed on his upper lip and then drops from his brow stung his eyes. The ecstasy continued to build. When he thought he could not stand any more, it increased so that he began to gulp deep breaths. He was in such a state that Satan had complete control of his soul and he cared not. Then a release was reached, a much better one this time. He screamed savagely for what seemed to be a long time. His heart was pounding rapidly and through his half-closed eyes he noticed the movement of the girl getting up. Soon the presence of Satan became real and a great feeling of depression began to take him over. He wanted to get up and run, but he was too weak. His heart pounded so that it echoed loudly in his ears and his sweater was soaked through. Could he be dying he wondered with a sudden panic? He would have no chance to confess this grievous sin and could end up in Hell for eternity. He had trouble gaining his breath. His heart had never acted as such. "Oh, God!" he cried aloud. He was afraid in this state of sin. Quickly, he recited an Act of Contrition to himself to return to a State of Grace. But then his heart began to slow down. Soon, it became apparent that he was not in mortal danger. He lay back on the couch and said nothing. He found himself surprisingly immodest with the uncovered portion of his body as the girl moved around somewhere behind him.

After some time his system had returned to a relative calmer state. He may have even fallen asleep for a short period. His arrogance was returning. He turned over his shoulder and said in a superior tone to the girl, "I need to leave. Where are my pants?"

A few moments later the whore draped them over the back of the couch with the soiled underwear on top. Regardless of their condition, he slipped them back on. Five minutes later Sadak was in his car on his way back to the rectory. He had already begun to rationalize that the girl and the Devil were one and the same. It was no wonder he had fallen. Who wouldn't have, after all? But he was now confident that this unfortunate episode would strengthen him ever so more for his Lord's work. He would confess this sin rightly and be through with it. And no mortal would be the wiser. So he thought.

CHAPTER 31

The next morning, at about the time Father Chester Sadak had said the early mass at a parish church with another Act of Contrition before changing the hosts and wine, Tom Baker walked into the coaches' office at Malloy High School. Baker knew that Frank O'Brien showed up early each morning and he wanted to talk to him with no one else around.

"Hey, Coach. How's it going?" The young former backfield coach said sheepishly.

O'Brien looked up from his practice charts. "Hello, Tom." He got up and they shook hands.

"I've been meaning to get by, but it's been pretty busy."

O'Brien nodded, figuring that what he meant by 'busy' was crying in his beer at the bars. The kid had put on quite a few pounds since summer and his ruddy face was puffy with blood shot eyes.

"You guys are having a great year. I wish I was part of it."

"I do too Tom. We could use you."

Baker laughed. "You've won every game by at least three touchdowns."

"The toughest are yet to come."

"You get by the next game and you're in the City Championship."

"Easier said than done."

The young man was silent for several moments, which led O'Brien to wonder the reason for his former assistant coach's visit. He had heard that the kid was getting soaked by an attorney. That had to cost him a grand. Maybe more.

"I've got a couple of job possibilities. Wanted to see if you can give me a good word."

"Coaching?"

"Yeah, up in Wisconsin."

"Sure. Have 'em give me a call."

"Thanks. I appreciate it with all that's happened."

"Sure." He said nothing further hoping the kid would leave before anyone came by.

"Thanks again." He extended his hand and they shook. "I'll be at the game next week. I'd like to come down on the field and say hello to the guys, but maybe that wouldn't be a good idea." He left an opening for O'Brien to say otherwise.

"You're right. Probably not."

The former Malloy backfield coach nodded ruefully and left the office. O'Brien was now glad to be rid of him. He was winning in spite of the kid's loss. But Baker's stupidity could have cost Malloy its championship season. Though the team still needed a win this Sunday, O'Brien had no doubts about the coming game. This opponent couldn't stop Bonjanovich. Yes, Malloy would be in the championship, the coveted game that drew upwards of a hundred thousand at Soldier Field. No, Baker wouldn't get a good word from him. He had let his head coach down, and for that he might as well just join the Army.

CHAPTER 32

"I'm worried, Mike," Johnny Costello whispered at the lunch table.

"Why?" Bonjanovich replied biting into a juicy Italian Beef Sandwich. His eyes surveyed the lunchroom as he chewed.

"You know why. These guys mean business."

"We'd be arrested by now if they had anything. Just keep your mouth shut and forget about it."

"I couldn't sleep last night. I can't concentrate in class."

Bonjanovich set his sandwich down. "Listen, Sunday's game means getting into the championship. I don't want to have to worry if the damn ball's going get in my hands on time."

"Oh no, Mike," Costello said quickly. "I won't have any trouble with football. It's the other stuff."

"You better not." He returned to the thick sandwich as Al Wasko, the fullback, approached the table with his tray and noticed the fowl looks on his teammates faces.

"You guys pissed off about something?"

With his mouth full Bonjanovich shook his head.

Costello looked to his quarterback, and then said, "No, nobody's pissed off about anything."

Wasko shrugged his broad shoulders and went to another table.

On Sunday Malloy did gain its berth in the city championship game, but not without an uncharacteristic struggle. The offense sputtered throughout most of the game and there were harsh words among the players. Bonjanovich's tongue was unmercifully sharp, lashing out at the poor blocking. And Johnny Costello didn't escape the quarterback's wrath when a center snap was juggled by Bonjanovich. But at the end of the game Malloy was two touchdowns ahead and on its way to the coveted championship. Costello adored his quarterback even more. He felt that Mike's harsh words were what the team needed in this important game. Yes, it was truly what the team needed, even though his words stung terribly.

Indeed the big game against the public school champs was an important game for a number of people. A win there would guarantee O'Brien a college job and Jack Stone figured he wouldn't be far behind. It would assure Costello and Wasko along with several of their team mates college scholarships. Bonjanovich, of course, had no worries about a scholarship, but the game would determine the measure of cash and other gifts both he and his father could expect. With the exception of a slight blip in his offense everything was falling into place for O'Brien. He went to bed that Sunday with no worries. The public school opponent was a poor representative and would be crushed easily by his Malloy squad. Perhaps by as much as six touchdowns. He slept well that night. It would be his last good night sleep for some time.

CHAPTER 33

Mike Bonjanovich spoke erroneously when he had implied that he and Costello had nothing to worry about with the deaths of the boys. The detectives had been side tracked for several days with the case of a young man who had turned up dead in an oil drum in an alley near Augusta Avenue. By that morning, when the halls of Malloy were abuzz about the great win the previous day, the detectives had solved the case and were ready to move on the two boys. Sheehan placed a call to Father Sobykevich before coming over. Having listened to the detective's reasons with distress, the principal assured him the boys would be present when they arrived and then ordered Wanda to fetch the pair.

When Bonjanovich and Costello were pulled from physics lab, it was assumed by their classmates that they were to be interviewed by the TV stations. A camera van from one of the stations in front of the school had not gone unnoticed. As fate was moving toward the boys, Frank O'Brien was glorifying his team, his staff and himself to the reporter under the stone façade at the entrance to the school.

Johnny Costello's eyes grew large when he saw the detectives enter the conference room. He was seated next to the quarterback and had been ranting about the game. Bonjanovich's only reaction was a look of disgust.

Fazio took a chair at the end of the table near Costello while Sheehan sat across from the two boys. Father Sobykevich entered last and sat two chairs down from Sheehan.

"You boys probably know why we're here," Sheehan started out. "You're both young and getting started in life, so we wanted to give you a chance to think about this matter."

"Last week we gave you a chance to talk about it," Fazio added. "We haven't heard anything, but it still isn't too late."

The detectives waited, but the boys said nothing.

"Okay," Sheehan sighed. "Why don't we go to the station where we can talk more about this? Father, I think you will need to call the boy's parents."

But before the principal could reply, Bonjanovich said, "You asked if we remembered where we were that morning."

Sheehan raised his eyebrows in surprise, "Yes."

"I thought about it and I remember that I went to breakfast with one of our priests that morning, Father Sadak."

Johnny's eyes widened and his mouth opened slightly while Father Sobykevich leaned forward with interest. He was about to say something but caught himself as he realized that it was the detective's place to speak.

"Really?" Sheehan said and exchanged looks with his partner.

Sheehan asked the principal, "Is it possible to have Father Sadak come here?"

He nodded and went to the door to ask Wanda to promptly find the priest. The principal returned to his chair and sat in an awkward silence with the detectives and the two students for a several minutes until Father indignantly swept into the room and glanced at the faces trained on him. Neither detective, nor the others rose when he entered.

"I was in the middle of an important lesson, Father. Why, may I ask, was I interrupted?"

"Father, these men are detectives and they need to ask you

some questions."

"Questions? I usually ask the questions," he smiled with a poor attempt at humor.

"Have a seat, Father," Fazio said, indicating a chair at the end of the table.

Sheehan looked over his notes and asked Sadak, "Do you recall having breakfast with Mike Bonjanovich on the second Saturday in October?"

The priest avoided looking at the school's star athlete. It was just after the night with that wretched woman that Bonjanovich had confronted him. It was incredible that he had somehow found out about the regrettable incident and was now openly blackmailing him, a man of God. He cocked his head with his eyes on the ceiling and made a show of thinking back. Then he did some silent counting with his fingers.

"Saturday, Saturday," he mumbled to himself. "Ah, yes. That Saturday. Yes, yes, we did have breakfast on what I believe was the eleventh. And most enjoyable it was."

The principal removed his glasses and anxiously cleaned them with a cotton cloth he had taken from his cassock.

"You did?" Fazio asked mildly. " What sort of things did you discuss?"

The shameless priest turned to his principal. "Really, Father. Must I answer any more of these ridiculous questions? My students are alone."

"Is there a reason not to, Father?"

"No, I suppose not." He turned to Fazio and replied, "Just school things. We might have talked about his game of football also."

"I see," the detective said with his dark eyes on the priest for several moments. He then looked at his partner who nodded a silent agreement.

"Okay Father, we don't have any more questions."

"Thank you," Father Sadak said and smugly stood up. He actually raised his chin at the detectives and carried himself summarily from the office.

Sheehan said to the quarterback, "Okay, Bonjanovich. You're free to go."

Fazio stopped Costello who had started to rise also from his chair along with his quarterback. "Johnny, we want to talk with you further."

Costello tensed as he sat back down while his teammate stood smugly with his hands on the back of the center's chair. Then he meaningfully squeezed Johnny's shoulder with the powerful right hand and looked him squarely in the eye as the boy looked up at his quarterback. It all became crystal clear to Johnny Costello. The great Bonjanovich, perhaps the greatest player ever to wear a Malloy jersey, must be protected; protected at least through the championship game. The success of the team was paramount and Mike's presence on the field was essential for such a triumph. A center was expendable. The center behind Johnny was not all that bad. But there was no replacement for Mike. Costello now understood his obligation to the team, to the coaches and to Malloy High School.

With Bonjanovich gone the detectives relaxed in their chairs a few moments while the principal dejectedly looked at his folded hands on the table. He was sure that Father Sadak had just lied to the police, as he was sure that Mike Bonjanovich had somehow coerced him into doing so. The fact that the senior athlete and Father Chester would have breakfast together on a

Saturday morning was about as likely as the principal converting to Judaism. Then he looked at young Costello trying to hide with a hard face just how frightened he was. At that moment the Father Principal prayed to God for enough strength to bear what was to come from all of this.

"You want to tell us what happened, Johnny?" Fazio asked quietly.

The boy began to rub his hands together nervously until the knuckles whitened. He stared at them in the silent room. After a while he said, "Yeah, I did it. I was there alone and I did it."

"You did what, Johnny?" Fazio asked quietly.

"I threw the burning shingle and killed them."

No one spoke as the admission took hold. A sound like a whimper came from Johnny's throat and he desperately fought back the urge to cry.

"Johnny, we didn't ask you if you were alone. Why did you say it?"

He shrugged his shoulders. "I don't know. I just did."

"Mike wasn't with you?" Sheehan asked.

He shook his head. "No, I said I was alone."

"Johnny," the other detective said, "we understand that you and Mike are good friends. He lives in Oak Park and you don't. Why would you be there by yourself?"

"I just was," he replied loudly. "Isn't that enough?"

Fazio sighed. "Did you do it on purpose?"

"No!" the boy sobbed. He rubbed his face with the sleeve of his shirt. "Now look what I've done. I can't be crying."

"How did it happen?" Sheehan inquired.

He wiped his face clear and said, "I just threw it for the hell of it and it just...it just went up." He couldn't control himself any longer and he began to cry openly.

Father Sobykevich stood and went over to the boy and put his hand on the shoulder Mike had pressured earlier, but for entirely different reasons. He lent the boy his hankie and Johnny wiped the tears from his face.

"What happens now?" the principal asked the detectives.

"We'll have to arrest him," Fazio answered. "His parents can post bail once he's arraigned."

"I'll call them," he said to his senior student and Johnny nodded.

The detectives got up and Fazio said, "Let's go son."

CHAPTER 34

The detectives led Johnny handcuffed through the front door past a cameraman and a reporter who was interviewing Frank O'Brien for the upcoming championship game.

"Where are you going?" the coach half-jokingly asked his center as he passed. He hadn't noticed the cuffed hands behind his back.

Johnny looked up but didn't answer his coach while the reporter, who had started out on the police beat, immediately recognized an arrest situation. He nudged his cameraman to follow him and they left O'Brien standing by himself.

"Is this student being arrested?" the reporter called out to the detectives who were moving quickly toward their unmarked car. They ignored him.

"You're on the football team, aren't you?" the reporter said trying desperately to get his microphone in front of the boy. Johnny didn't answer him, but his look said that the reporter had guessed correctly.

"What is he being arrested for?" he impatiently asked Fazio who was closest to him.

Leaving the question unanswered, Fazio maneuvered the boy into the back seat of the car and went around front to join his partner who had already started the engine. The camera followed them as they pulled from the curb with Johnny's face turned away. He had earlier dreamed of gaining some of the attention that Mike had been enjoying, but was now hiding his face like mobsters he had often seen on television.

Once the police car was out of sight, the reporter looked for Frank O'Brien, but the coach had already disappeared back inside the school building.

CHAPTER 35

Al Costello's hasty steps toward the precinct house were comical to watch. With straight legs and a backward lean to the side to counterbalance an immense beer gut, he moved toward the old building at a near-run. What was this nonsense about Johnny being arrested he angrily thought? Had Johnny and Mike gotten into a fight with some kids? Father John...whatever the hell the Polock's last name is...said it was serious. This is a hell of time, the biggest week of his boy's life, to be causing any distractions. Costello had a couple of beers with two more on the way at the bar when work called him about the arrest. He wished he had taken those with him. He'd have a few things to say to these no good cops.

"Detective Sheehan," he wheezed to the sergeant at the front desk. Though it was a brisk day, Al's blue Park District shirt showed sweat rings down close to his waist.

The sergeant pointed to an iron stairway, which led up to the second floor of the station. Costello hustled up the stairs, hanging on to the rail with each step. There he found a bullpen of desks and walked swiftly up and down the floor until he saw a nameplate with 'Detective Sheehan' on it. A young man with reddish hair sat behind it with his tie loosened.

"I'm Al Costello. Where's my son?"

The detective looked at him for a moment, then stood and extended his hand, "Pat Sheehan." He added, "This is Detective Fazio," indicating a darker, older man at an adjoining desk. Fazio nodded at Al who gave him little attention.

"What's this all about? Johnny get into a fight with someone? We can take care of that now, can't we?"

He was implying some sort of a payoff.

"I'm afraid it's more involved than that," Sheehan told him, ignoring the suggested offer.

"More involved? What the shit does that mean? Don't you know that Johnny's playing in the City Championship on Saturday?"

"Why don't you have a seat, Mr. Costello," the detective offered patiently.

Al began to object but then dropped heavily onto the metal chair next to Sheehan's desk. By now his shirt was soaked through.

The detective sat back down and said, "Your son admitted to starting a fire that killed three boys."

"What!" Al scowled not really understanding what had just been said. Then he let out a nervous chuckle and sucked in some air. "Johnny doesn't go around starting fires. He plays football. He's got a big game Saturday, the biggest game of his life."

"There's no mistake," Sheehan said. "We interviewed him with Mike Bonjanovich earlier today and Johnny confessed. He said he was alone and did it himself."

"Confessed! That's crazy. You said Mike. What's he got to do with this stupid thing?"

"Mike and Johnny are pretty close, aren't they?" Fazio asked.

Al looked at the other detective, his shallow mind trying to calculate the situation.

"Sure, they're friends," he answered cautiously.

The detective was about to say something when Al started to nod knowingly.

"I get it! You think I was born yesterday? I'm with the City. I know how you bastards work. You were looking for a patsy and you forced Johnny into saying these things. And you're looking to lay the same thing on Mike. What the hell, you guys got money on the public school team? That's it. You want these guys out of the game Saturday."

The detectives looked at each other and held back smiles while Costello continued to rant, "Where is he? I want to see him."

"He's charged with a felony," Sheehan said leaning forward in his chair. "Only his attorney can see him right now."

"You mean I can't take him home with me? What kind of a deal is this?"

"Bail needs to be set at a hearing in the morning. He'll spend the night in jail," Fazio said.

"What about practice? He can't miss practice. What's it going to take?" He reached into his pocket and took out a folded wad of bills. "I said I know how this works," he cried, causing heads to turn from other desks at the crude offer of a bribe.

Sheehan said, "Put that money away and get Johnny an attorney, Mr. Costello. He's in jail charged with a felony."

Al held the money out for several moments, then nodded with narrowed eyes. "You can bet your ass I'll get an attorney. I'll get one all right and I'll have both of your goddamned badges." He stuffed the money back in his pocket with a few crumpled bills falling out to the floor and stormed away from the desk toward the stairway.

Sheehan looked over at his partner. "Aren't you proud to be a fellow City employee to Al?"

"He's a real treat. I feel sorry for the kid. He's going to need a lot of help and he's not going to get it there."

Sheehan leaned back in his chair. "I guess right now I just feel sorry for the three kids and their families and I'd like to figure out how we can get to Bonjanovich."

His partner nodded and agreed, "Yeah."

CHAPTER 36

Frank O'Brien took a clipboard in his hand and smashed it down hard against the corner of his desk. Cheap wood splintered in all directions and the sound resonated through the office and gymnasium. Jack Stone flinched at his desk.

"Everything we've worked for is about to happen and now we don't have a goddamned center."

"What happened to Johnny?" Stone asked.

"All I know is the idiot got arrested for starting a fire in some prairie," he lashed out at his line coach.

"Arrested! For starting a fire in a prairie? That can't be so bad," Stone replied.

"They say three kids died in it."

"Jesus!"

The head coach flung the remains of the board against the wall.

"Can you get Palumbo ready by Saturday?" he asked Stone.

"What?" he said with his thoughts on his senior center who was at the moment behind bars.

"Palumbo. Our second string center."

"Oh sure. He'll be ready. What about Bonjanovich?"

"Bonjanovich. What about him?" O'Brien's patience was thin.

"Costello sticks to him like glue. And I hear they were both called to the office earlier today."

O'Brien stared at his line coach with his mouth opened

slightly. "Mike wasn't arrested," he snapped.

"That's good," he said more to himself. "I was just wondering."

"Don't wonder anymore, okay?"

"Sure," he said in an offhanded tone.

O'Brien contemplated a few moments, and then said, "There's a freshman named Sikorski who pointed Costello out. You know him?"

"Sikorski?" Stone thought a moment and said, "Yeah, he's in my history class."

"What's he like?"

"I don't know. Quiet I guess. Smart as hell." He waited for more, but O'Brien kept to his thoughts. "Get'em started stretching. I've got to make a couple of calls."

"Okay," Stone replied and left the office.

The head coach closed the door after him and looked up Nick Bonjanovich's number on his rolodex.

"Nick? Frank O'Brien here."

"Yeah, Frank. How's it going?"

"We've got a problem here and Mike could be involved."

Nick Bonjanovich quietly listened to O'Brien go over the story that would soon be on the news. After he was through, there was a long silence. Then Bonjanovich asked," You say the kid's name is Sikorski?"

"His first name's Andrew."

"Thanks, Frank." The line went dead and O'Brien began to have second thoughts about mentioning the kid to Nick. Then he thought to himself, the hell with it. The kid should know enough to keep his mouth shut. He rose to join the team at practice.

CHAPTER 37

Tina Costello was busy fixing a pot roast for her boys when Al barged through the back door. For the past couple of hours he had been looking for Danny O'Shea, his cousin the lawyer, but Danny had proved difficult to locate. He thought of him at once upon leaving the police station. For a family member Danny would surely give a break on his fee. He searched for Danny at bars he was known to frequent, and Al, of course, had a quick taste at each establishment to steady his nerves. He came home without locating the lawyer and was loaded to boot.

"Hello Al," Tina chirped in a sing-song voice. "Is my Johnny not far behind? I have dinner ready for my growing boys." She was just starting to mash the potatoes.

Al roughly pulled out a kitchen drawer and started to rummage through some papers.

"Johnny's in jail. Where's the goddamn number for that shyster Danny O'Shea."

Tina Costello dropped the masher into the potatoes and stepped back holding her cheeks in her hands.

"Jail! What…?"

"O'Shea's number. Where is it?"

She couldn't answer him. She couldn't think. Her head shook violently and she started to scream.

Costello held his wife's flabby arms and yelled, "Shut up! I need the lawyer's number."

She could as much have found O'Shea's number at that

moment as she could have recited the entire Chicago Yellow Pages from memory. Instead, she screamed pitifully louder with large bulging eyes. Costello pulled away from his wife in disgust and continued to search through the drawer until he found the number and dialed it.

"Al Costello here, Judy," he said into the phone... " You know, Danny's cousin. You remember me from the Fourth of July picnic." The snooty bitch that wouldn't give him the time of day, Costello thought. "Say, Judy, I need Danny. Is he there?" He tried to sound casual, as if he was used to talking business with his cousin. Next to him with her head in her hands, Tina stood whimpering.

"When he gets in have, him call me. It's important."

He gave her the number and hung up.

"Whaa...what happened?" Tina cried and started to sob loudly, gulping large amounts of air.

"Stop crying for Christ's sake. I can't think with you blubbering like that."

He wanted to slap her and he raised his hand. Her sobs grew into convulsive gasps and he dropped his hand.

"Cut it out, Tina," Al yelled, spewing boozy breath into his wife's face. "Johnny might be in jail for a speeding ticket and you're hysterical about it."

"But...a lawyer!"

"That's right. He needs a lawyer. The week of the championship game when every college coach in the country will be in the stands. I'm going to look for O'Shea. Get a message if he calls."

"But what will I tell him?"

Instead of answering her, he abruptly left the house. As fast as Al had appeared when Tina's world was bright and bubbly, he was gone, leaving her in a weeping clump against the wall without even a clue as to what had happened to her dear Johnny. He was in a jail cell somewhere in Chicago for some unknown reason. The potatoes and roast began to burn.

CHAPTER 38

D anny O'Shea finally got back with his cousin at 8:30 the next morning. He received the message late the night before at a time he often received most of his messages and figured he shouldn't be returning calls at such an hour.

"How's my favorite cousin?" O'Shea bellowed through the phone. His eyes were red like Costello's normally were, but a slight hangover was a matter of course for the lawyer. He felt great and was ready for the day.

"Where the hell have you been?" Al barked into the kitchen phone. "My kid got into trouble, Danny. He's in jail". Al was wearing crusty boxer shorts and a sleeveless T-shirt from the night before.

O'Shea hated to be called Danny. It was what his asshole cousin had called him as a kid and continued to do so as they got older when everyone else referred to him properly as Daniel. "What'd he do, Al?" he asked bracing up a bit.

"Something about a fire. I think it's all trumped up."

"A fire. What kind? Anybody hurt?'

"Yeah. Three kids got killed, but like I say, it's all a bunch of malarkey."

A gasp came from another room. It was the first Tina had seen of her husband since the evening before, and she had stayed awake throughout the night without a clue as to where her son was being held or for what reason.

"Christ. That's not good," the lawyer said squirting some

breathe sweetener into his mouth. "What precinct's he at?"

"Austin. There's a couple of jerk cops there. You gonna get him out now?"

"There's got to be a hearing for something like that, Al."

"What's it gonna cost to get him off, Danny? A couple hundred maybe?"

The lawyer thought for a few moments. "It's not going to be that easy. Kids were killed and Johnny's a ballplayer. The press might be in on it."

"The hell with the press. Johnny's got to be in Soldier Field on Saturday. The team needs him, so find a way to get him out."

O"Shea sighed. "Meet me at the precinct at eleven."

"Can't you get there earlier?"

"I've got some appointments."

Costello started to say something about an appointment with a glass of Irish whiskey, but then caught himself as he needed the lawyer's help. "Okay." After he hung up, Tina appeared in a robe from the next room. Her eyes were red and glassy.

"Johnny hurt somebody?" she asked Al in a weak voice. She couldn't bear to repeat what she had just heard and had actually erased the words from her thoughts with the hopes she had heard wrong.

Al wet a dishtowel and put it to his face. He avoided her question.

" I got to take a shower. Fix me some breakfast, will you?"

Tina wanted to demand more information, but the years of submission to Al led her to turn to the refrigerator to fetch some eggs for his breakfast.

CHAPTER 39

Nick Bonjanovich was alone in his tiny office twirling a paper cup containing a small amount of anisette. He sipped and thought. The Costello kid was in jail for burning some kids to death. His old man was a buffoon and would probably make matters worse for the kid rather than grease the wheels suitably so that he could play on Saturday. Too bad, but Malloy would still win without Johnny. What worried him was Mike's connection in the matter. He was questioned along with Costello, but he wasn't arrested. But for the last year that Costello kid was on Mike like stink on shit. Chances were that Mike was involved somehow. Mike was just cleverer than that hapless friend of his. But this kid Sikorski seemed to be an eyewitness and that could eventually spell trouble for Mike. He twirled his drink and thought about the kid. He needed information on him. He opened his desk drawer and found a slip of paper in a corner with only a phone number on it. He closed the drawer and dialed the number.

"Yeah," a raspy voice answered.

"Joe, this is Nick from the neighborhood."

After a short silence the voice said, "What can I do for you, Nick?"

"Mike might have some trouble. I need some information on a kid."

"Yeah."

He gave him what he knew about Andrew Sikorski and told him about the fire. Nick added that he would take care of his usual fee.

"How's Mikey doing?" Joe asked. "We're proud of him you know."

"He's going to be able to write his ticket. As long as this thing doesn't blow up."

The voice waited, and then offered. "If this kid's a real problem to Mikey, I'd be glad to take care of him. No extra charge. Mikey's a good boy."

Nick was silent for a while drumming the fingers of his free hand on the desk. "Thanks. Let me think about that."

"I'll get back with you in a couple of days."

The line went dead. Bonjanovich hung the phone up and picked the cup back up. He swirled and watched the clear liquor in thought and then finished it off in one drink snapping back his head.

CHAPTER 40

The persecution of Andrew Sikorski began during the lunch period in which the seniors and freshmen ate together. Johnny Costello was one of their own and the hype of the coming championship game already had the seniors at a fever pitch. Irrespective of the fact that three boys had died horribly in the fire, and that Sikorski had been found and pressed to talk by the police, Andrew was still looked upon as a lowly snitch.

A third string halfback was the first to approach the apprehensive freshman at his table.

"This school's not for squealers," the squat boy with pimples and fuzz on his chin said, standing with fists half closed at his sides. Sikorski stared ahead and said nothing and the senior moved along when the new lunchroom proctor, a meek quiet individual, looked up from his breviary.

The barbs continued and became more vicious. A tall, rangy senior walked up to Andrew at his locker and said from the side of his mouth without looking at him, "We'll cut off your balls you little prick."

In class, a number of seniors would stop by his room and stare at him in his seat. By the end of the day the junior and sophomore classes had picked up the lead so that Andrew couldn't escape from being ostracized. After school he went straight home, foregoing his usual meeting with the Electronics Club. He avoided Tony as much as possible as he didn't want to talk about this horrible matter. He just wanted out of his miserable school and to be away from all of these people. No sooner had he stepped through the door at home and a vulgar threatening call came. He laid the phone off the hook and went upstairs to lie down.

CHAPTER 41

Johnny Costello had been in jail once before in his life. A couple of years back several of the boys from the neighborhood were caught trespassing in the ruins of a mansion north of Chicago which was once a hideout for the gangster, Al Capone. It was before Johnny started to run with Mike Bonjanovich. The boys were locked up in cells of a ritzy suburban jail with freshly painted walls and comfortable varnished benches. They knew that they would be out soon and they made the most of it as a lark.

Costello thought back to that night. Knowing that they'd soon be free gave them a brash boldness. They had put away a few beers and had some fun with the suburban cops who wore fitted tan shirts and ties. The boys were tough guys from Chicago, they thought. A couple made fun of the cops from their cushy cells. It turned out to be a grand night that they would talk about for some time. That was quite a time, Costello thought. Unlike this horror. He forced himself not to look at his cell mate. The man sat, hunched up with thin arms covered by tattoos, starring with dark fixed eyes at the high school senior. Figuring that the boy was still in school he had earlier asked if he could get ahold of any drugs in the chemistry lab. He frightened Johnny, and the boy wouldn't let himself fall to sleep in the dank cell that smelled miserably of stale urine.

The day stretched on unbearably until he was finally brought before a judge in handcuffs at 3:00 that afternoon, the precise time the team would start practice. Waiting for him in a small hearing room with a judge was his father, his Uncle Danny and the two detectives who had arrested him. His father hadn't shaved and smelled of booze. Also present were a couple of reporters, standing to the side with notepads open.

"Hello, Johnny," O'Shea said with a grim smile, putting a trusting hand on the boy's shoulder.

"Hi Uncle Danny, he replied weakly. He started to put a hand forward then remembered that they were restrained. His father said nothing.

O'Shea put on a more serious face. "They say you've gotten into some trouble son."

"Yes, sir," the boy answered looking down. His lawyer patted him again on the shoulder, this time in a more sympathetic manner.

The judge, a gray-haired Irishman, cleared his throat with his eyes on the police reports in front of him. He shifted his glasses as he read. Finally, he looked up at Johnny.

"You told the detectives that you started the fire in which three boys died?"

Johnny nodded.

"Your Honor," O'Shea broke in "It was an accident."

The judge put up the palm of his hand.

"Did you know the boys were inside the wood structure when you threw the shingles at it?"

Johnny shook his head.

The judge looked at the report further.

"It says another boy was seen with you, a Mike Bonjanovich. Is that true, son?" The judge asked.

Johnny glanced at the reporters. He shook his head.

The mention of the great quarterback caused the reporters to stir. Al moved from his place behind O'Shea and Johnny. In his drunken state Al had forgotten about the mention of Mike's involvement. This was his boy's out, he figured, and he wouldn't have to pay much to his shyster cousin. He stepped forward and said, "Johnny, tell them that Mike was with you!"

"Son," the judge prompted. "This is a very serious matter. You say it was an accident. Accidents happen, but you need to be completely truthful with the court."

"Yes, sir," Johnny murmured. But he volunteered nothing further. He wouldn't be the cause Mike missing the big game.

The judge studied him a moment then, shaking his head, proclaimed, "This case will be sent to the grand jury." He pounded his gavel.

Johnny turned anxiously to his uncle. "What does that mean?"

The lawyer raised his hand to imply that the boy shouldn't worry.

"The matter of bail, your Honor?" the lawyer asked.

"Twenty thousand dollars."

Johnny gasped with fear that he would need to return to that cell.

"That means we must put up two thousand. It's a simple matter," O'Shea assured his nephew.

Instead of going to his son, Al Costello approached the detectives. "Why didn't you arrest Mike?"

"He had an alibi," Sheehan answered, tired of the elder Costello.

"If he has an alibi, so does Johnny. Johnny wouldn't be out there without Mike."

"Maybe not. But your son confessed that he was alone."

O'Shea interrupted them. "They're taking Johnny to the bondsman. We can meet him there."

Costello had more to say to the detectives, but they had quickly left the room. The reporters followed the Costellos and the lawyer.

CHAPTER 42

After he had dropped Johnny off with the boy's weeping mother, Al started out for the Malloy practice field to find Nick. On the way he figured that he could use a little support after all he had gone through and stopped at one of the taverns he normally frequented. When he arrived at practice, the team was in a full scrimmage against a light swirl of snowflakes from a front that had blown in from the north. Dressed in an open windbreaker with his prominent belly, Al marched up and down the sideline looking for Bonjanovich, but he was nowhere to be found. The other fathers made no attempt to speak to Al. A couple nodded when he caught their glances. Most avoided eye contact, pretending to concentrate on the scrimmage, but all knew well that he was present.

On the field Mike was running the offense, as photographers were active snapping pictures. They hustled from place to place to shoot a variety of angles. Al noticed that Mike was taking snaps from the sophomore center like nothing had happened; as if Johnny had never been there to lead the way for him. Frustrated, Al was about to leave to look for Nick elsewhere when a reporter stopped him.

"Aren't you Johnny Costello's father?" the short squat man in a wide brimmed hat with a wool sweater under a wrinkled trench coat asked.

Al looked at him with bloodshot eyes and said nothing.

Flipping open his note pad, the reporter asked, "Coach O'Brien said Johnny most likely won't play in the championship game. Is that true?"

Al waved the question away brusquely. "That's all a bunch of horse shit!"

"But isn't your boy in jail?"

Al's face reddened. He had seen the reporter before at practice. He was with one of the papers and Al was the proud father when the man had asked Johnny a few questions earlier in the year. But all of that had changed as Al now despised the nosy runt.

"Leave me alone. It's none of your goddamned business!"

But the determined reporter continued, "It's stated that Johnny was involved in the fire that killed three boys in Oak Park? It's a serious charge. What can you say about that, Mr. Costello?"

Al clenched his teeth and grabbed the pad from the reporter's hands and pitched it into the wind toward the playing field. The pages flapped wildly before it dropped onto the ground. The reporter calmly stepped out onto the field to pick the pad up and shook it free from dirt. Al clenched his fists hoping the reporter would give him some lip so that he could lay into him, but the man only looked at him oddly. Al turned and saw that all of the team fathers, all pals at one time, were staring at him.

"What are you looking at?" he spit out furiously and then stomped from the field.

A few minutes later he was at a pay phone on North Avenue. He yelled over the street traffic, "It's Al, Connie. I need to talk to Nick."

Connie said that he wasn't home. Her voice was hard for Al to hear with the blowing cold wind and the traffic. "What did you say?"

"He's not here."

"Where the hell is he?" he screamed. "It's important."

Connie didn't know and offered no suggestions. Life with her husband and her son had made her very careful with her words.

"What time will he be home?"

She didn't know that either.

"What the hell do you know, Connie?"

She said nothing.

"Come on Connie," he cried out pathetically. "We're friends, aren't we? Where's he at?"

She told Al only that she would let Nick know he had called and the line went dead.

"No good bitch!" he yelled and slammed the receiver against the side of the booth, cracking the glass.

CHAPTER 43

It was particularly courageous of Andrew to attend school the next day, considering the abuse he had already endured. Perhaps, he figured that the older students would tire of such nonsense, but regrettably, there was no let up in the persecution. Even his fellow freshmen, especially those playing football, had now joined in the fray.

Such appalling treatment of his friend caused Tony to become livid. With the matter of Brother Vladimir still a fresh memory, the freshman quieted down when Tony was near Andrew. The seniors, however, paid little attention to the reputation of a freshman, and their vicious barbs continued.

The day before Andrew wanted nothing to do with Tony or anyone else. Today his friend's support was welcomed. By lunch he thought that he might even make it through the day unscathed. But, when the lunchroom proctor's back was turned a tomato sailed across the room from a senior table and caught the boy in the face. His glasses broke at the stem and crashed to the floor. A spontaneous uproar followed.

Barbini was outraged as Andrew began to sob openly. He got up and pulled his friend with him. He took him through the lunchroom past the new proctor amidst cruel catcalls from the seniors and up the stairs to the principal's office. So angry was Barbini that he passed Wanda and took Andrew with tomato drippings on his face and shirt straight into Father Sobykevich's office.

"Father, terrible things are happening to Andy and it has to stop!"

Sensing at once that this had to do the Costello affair, the principal rose quickly from his chair.

"What happened?" he asked with a measure of anger beginning to build.

"Andy did what he was supposed to and everyone in the school hates him for it."

"How long has this been going on?" he asked Andrew as the boy tried to wipe his face clean with his sleeve.

Andrew answered with embarrassment, "Since Johnny Costello was arrested."

"I'm sorry Andrew. There's no excuse for this sort of behavior. I'll take care of this right now."

And he did. Father John called an immediate assembly of the entire student body in the gym.

As with any impromptu assembly there was a good deal of buzzing among the students. Each class sat in separate sections with the seniors up front with the best view. The principle stood grimly behind a microphone with his hands on his hips staring until the noise lessened and then completely disappeared. He let the silence take its affect until the rumble of the heating unit and maybe a few coughs became the only sound in the gym.

"A disturbing matter has come to my attention," he finally said in an exact voice. "It's no secret that the police have been investigating a tragic matter involving one or more of our students. One has been arrested. It is now up to our legal system to determine the truth in this matter. This is all very unsettling. The lives of three boys, the ages of some of your brothers and sisters, were lost." He paused and stared directly at the members of the senior class. Then he continued with a rising voice, "But what is more disconcerting is that many of you have taunted and threatened a young boy, one of your fellow students, who was simply asked by the police to tell the truth. Not to lie!" He pointed in the direction of the area where confessional booths were set up during mass. "Simply to follow one of God's sacred commandments." His face reddened. He took a deep breath and blasted into the microphone, "If I hear of one more instance of that boy or any other boy being threatened, that person will be immediately expelled and, so help me God, you'll never again see the inside of Malloy High School!"

He turned abruptly and left the gym. Left was the echo of his voice and a stunned student body that remained still for a long while.

It was Bonjanovich who first got up and arrogantly walked from the gym. A few seniors followed suit, but the rest of the student body was slow to break ranks.

Frank O'Brien stood by his office door where he had listened to the principal's talk and watched his quarterback leave the gym with a look of obvious resentment. This Costello matter was indeed becoming quite complicated. But it was not the senior center in his thoughts at the moment. Instead he was giving thought to Coach Stone and he smiled with the idea that had formed. His success hadn't come by accident, had it? Yes, Frank O'Brien was one to meticulously prepare his state of affairs both on and off the field.

CHAPTER 44

On his bus ride home from school Andrew tried to take stock in the day's events. He was tired but unable to rest. Had the words of the principal quashed the dreadful treatment he had been receiving from the students? No longer was he being harassed, but neither did he see many smiles since the assembly. Tony came to mind and Andrew began to appreciate just how much courage the boy had. He was also so persistent in pursuing a friendship, which Andrew for some reason insisted on discouraging. He was now glad for the boy's perseverance.

The amount of courage shown by his father in New Mexico was also becoming more apparent to Andrew. It was not a pleasant experience to be ostracized by those around you. And then the added pressure of losing a job and a career with a family to support must have been horrible.

What would tomorrow bring, he wondered? He felt sorry for Johnny Costello who must be living in a nightmare at the moment. He was no longer afraid of this sad boy, but Mike Bonjanovich still frightened him. There was something about the star football player that wasn't quite right. Andrew didn't fully understand his reasoning, but none the less, he was scared.

Andrew stepped down from the bus when it had reached his stop and crossed the street for his walk home. He didn't notice the man with a dark complexion in a nearby car watching him.

CHAPTER 45

Jack Barbini was sipping coffee thoughtfully in his office at the Town Hall precinct. His thoughts were on what was being crudely referred to in police talk at the Austin Precinct as the 'snapper-burner' case, referring to the high school center charged with the burning deaths of the three boys. When he became aware that the prime witness in the case, that may well involve Mike Bonjanovich, was the good friend of his son, his interest perked. Jack Barbini knew well the quarterback's old man. Though Nick Bonjanovich was small potatoes in Chicago mob circles, he could be a dangerous person. He bit off the end of a new cigar and wetted it with his mouth while he continued to think the matter through. After a few minutes the captain punched an intercom button on his desk and spoke to a secretary. "Send John Harnett in here."

A muffled voice squawked an affirmative response and a couple of minutes later a burly young man with cropped hair came through the door. He wore a flannel shirt over a thermal underwear shirt. The sleeves of the shirt were rolled up revealing strong forearms.

"Captain," the undercover cop greeted his boss.

"Harnett, I want you to keep an eye on someone for a few days. It has to do with a case over at Austin."

Harnett nodded and took a chair to listen to what the captain had to say.

CHAPTER 46

A fine practice had just finished and Frank O'Brien was in a particularly good mood. The sophomore center was working out. The kid was scared all right, but that wasn't bad. Some fear was expected and would be good for an underclassman as it kept him sharp. But it had to be under control. Especially at center, otherwise the snap might be all over the place. O'Brien had also been worried about the friendship between Bonjanovich and Costello. He knew they hung around together, though he wasn't quite sure why. But the kid being put away in jail didn't seem to bother his quarterback terribly, which was pleasing to the coach.

A man in a wrinkled trench coat and a brimmed hat appeared in the doorway to the coaches' office. It was the reporter who had had his notepad tossed by Al Costello.

"Coach O'Brien, any word on Johnny Costello? Have you talked with him?"

"His legal representation has recommended that we not contact Johnny until this is over," he lied. He had heard that Johnny's uncle hadn't talked with the boy since the bail hearing. For that matter no one had.

The reporter wrote this down which irritated O'Brien.

Then he paused. "Could Mike Bonjanovich also be arrested for the Oak Park fire?"

O'Brien shoved his desk forward and got up in the same motion.

"What makes you say something like that?" He pointed a

finger at the reporter who had taken a step back. "You better not print any of that crap!"

The reporter coolly asked, "You didn't answer. Could it happen?"

For a moment it seemed as if O'Brien might grab the man by the throat. Then he backed off and calmed down some.

"Could it happen? Could the sun set to the East? Of course it couldn't happen. Mike was with one of the priests that morning."

"He was?" the reporter responded with surprise.

"That's right. I understand they had breakfast together. You going to write that down?" he said motioning to the reporter's pad.

He folded the pad and bit the side of his lip. "I guess that's all then."

"I guess so," O'Brien mimicked.

He nodded and then left. The head coach pushed his desk back into place and thought about his quarterback. A minute later, Jack Stone entered his office, perspiring freely under a wet suit. He had joined the team in its conditioning run and had stopped by the weight room on his way in. O'Brien watched his line coach peel off the wet suit in the locker room doorway, allowing a sizable amount of body water to splash on the floor by the drain.

"Good workout, Coach Stone?" he inquired lightly.

"Yeah. It's a good release."

O"Brien stretched with a yawn. "God knows we need it now."

Stone paused. "After so many years, you still get nervous like this?"

With his hands interlocked behind his head, he joked, "If I

didn't, I wouldn't belong in this profession."

While Stone showered, Frank O'Brien thought again about his line coach. Owen Hollingsworth, the great coach from Nebraska State, was in town to look at Bonjanovich. He desperately needed a young run pass quarterback and had left an open invitation for dinner with O'Brien. But the Malloy coach had been slow to accept, as it was well known that Hollingsworth seldom had any openings on his staff and, when he did, he normally hired on one of his young graduates. With so many college coaches in town, O'Brien wanted to be prudent with his time for his own purposes. But now he had decided to take Hollingsworth up on his offer.

Stone stepped from the shower and was drying off when O'Brien said, "Owen Hollingsworth wants to get together at Fritzels for dinner. Can you make it?"

"Coach Hollingsworth!" Stone said looking up from a leg he was wiping dry. He was suddenly nervous at the prospect of dinner with such a famous coach. "When?"

"Tonight."

Stone tried to put his fears aside. "Sure, that sounds great."

"Good. I'll drive."

Jack Stone rapidly dried himself off as excitement filled his veins. Dinner with a legend! Is this how college jobs came about, he wondered? In an hour he would be across the table from the great Owen Hollingsworth. He wondered what he'd talk about. Stone generally felt at ease talking football, but Christ almighty, how could he talk the game with Coach Hollingsworth? He didn't know enough to talk at that level. He was becoming very nervous as he rubbed the towel hard at his skin.

CHAPTER 47

John Harnett held no sense of awe for famous athletes. He had been a ballplayer himself, lettering in three sports at De Paul Academy and was offered several college scholarships upon graduation. But after high school he had no further interest in sports or studying. He had a wild hair and joined the army. With his athletic skills and a keen mind, he was immediately selected to train for a newly formed Special Forces unit. Training was centered primarily on jungle warfare, and within a year he found himself in Southeast Asia advising local armies of governments favorable to the United States. A more subtle duty was the gathering of information for the intelligence community. After his tour, he felt uncomfortable with the political direction of the operation and decided not to re-up. Instead, he traveled for a while throughout Europe and then returned to Chicago to join the police department. His combat skills and intelligence experience made him a natural for undercover work, so that's where he found himself after only a few months with the Department.

Harnett was sipping a cup of coffee as he worked a crossword puzzle in a small café across the street from Nick Bonjanovich's office From his table he had a clear view of the office's front door, and at the same time he could see Bonjanovich's car parked at the end of the block. The cop had left his car on the same side of the street as Bonjanovich's when Nick went into his office earlier. A light snow began to fall dusting the street. Snow made stakeout work difficult. If it came down too hard, Hartnett would have to get out in it so he wouldn't miss his target. But a few minutes later the quarterback's father appeared in the narrow doorway to his office, wearing a tan leather car coat. He looked both ways then started off quickly toward the car. Harnett folded the paper and left the café to follow.

The drive took them west through Chicago toward the suburbs. Bonjanovich finally came to his destination in Stone Park, and the cop parked his car, an older Chevy with a big engine, on a nearby side street. Nick had entered a small limestone cottage style building that had been converted into a bar. When Hartnett entered through the front door, he found the bar empty except for two men in a booth and the bartender. The bartender was heavy set with dark unkempt hair. He motioned with his head to Hartnett who was dressed shabbily in his undercover attire. "Get out."

"I want a drink."

"Not here you don't," he answered.

"Why the hell not. I'm thirsty."

"This ain't no factory bar." He lifted a small club with a rawhide wrist strap from behind the bar. There was probably a gun down there somewhere also.

"All right, all right," Harnett relented. "I don't want no trouble for just a shot."

He left, but not before seeing the man with Bonjanovich.

In the booth Bonjanovich grimly watched the commotion at the bar. His eyes shifted to his friend from the old neighborhood, Joe Gatta.

"Garbage," Nick said. "He should've come across the bar and given the bum a good whack."

The other nodded and sipped anisette from a small narrow glass.

Nick's friend got right to it. "The kid's smart as hell. His old man's a college teacher. Used to make atomic bombs."

"They need money?" Bonjanovich asked. He was drinking scotch.

Gatta shrugged. "Got a house in Oak Park and he drives a new Buick."

Bonjanovich took a good drink from the scotch.

"Anything he doesn't want known?"

"He had a run in with FBI. They got him kicked out of the bomb work for not telling stories on one of his pals. Wife killed herself over it."

Bonjaovich said nothing.

"You got a father with a kid. If he thought something might happen to the kid, he'd probably put a clamp on him."

Bonjanovich nodded with understanding. "Let me get back with you on that."

He slipped an envelope, not unlike the ones he received from the colleges, from his jacket pocket and slid it across the table.

The man took the envelop and it disappeared under the table.

"Remember my offer. I want to see Mikey do good. If this kid might screw up his future, I'll take care of things."

"Thanks," Nick said and shook his hand before getting up.

The snow had stopped, making Bonjanovich easy to spot leaving the bar from even a block away. Fortunately, Harnett didn't have to wait long in his car at the edge of an open prairie. If a Stone Park cop came along, he'd probably have run the

Chicago detective off. Out here it wouldn't be a good idea to flash his Chicago badge, as he might just have been locked up for kicks. He ducked below the dashboard when Bonjanovich made a U-turn and drove by. He then waited for the other man to come out of the bar. John Hartnett recognized muscle when he saw it and decided to follow him.

CHAPTER 48

Owen Hollingsworth was at the bar in Fritzel's, a renowned downtown steakhouse, when the two high school coaches entered the restaurant. Hollingsworth actually bore little semblance to a football coach, hunched over with one foot on the brass rail in a lively discussion with an expensively dressed patron to his side. The coach was short and soft with a double chin. His hair was thin and he wore a tweed sport coat with suede patches on the elbows.

"Well, hello Frank," the famous coach announced when he caught eye of O'Brien. "Meet this good man who has given me some fine company tonight," he said indicating the man next to him.

O'Brien shook hands with the man and then Hollingsworth's. O'Brien then introduced Jack Stone to both and the handshakes were repeated.

"I hope we're not late," O'Brien said.

"Not at all, not at all. I always try to get to this delightful bar when I'm in Chicago."

"Well," he apologized to the patron, "it's time for some serious football talk." He laid a hand on the man's shoulder. "It's been a sincere pleasure."

The man gladly shook hands with Hollingsworth. It was a brief time in the life of the man who probably shook mountains in the business world, but he would repeat this meeting to anyone who would listen for years to come.

"So, Coach Stone," Hollingsworth said as they took their

seats at a table, "How does it feel to be in the big show."

To hear his name spoken by the prominent coach thrilled Jack, but he tried not to gush.

"It's great for the team," he replied modestly. "The boys worked hard for this."

Hollingsworth chuckled, rotating the martini he had brought from the bar. On the ring finger of each hand were huge bowl rings with diamonds.

"Surely sound coaching hasn't hurt any."

Stone smiled with some embarrassment.

"Coach Stone's done a terrific job with the line," O'Brien said with a glad hand to Stone's back.

Hollingsworth nodded thoughtfully and took small drink.

"I started out with the line. That's the part of the game I miss. The day to day work in the trenches."

"Nebraska State would be sorry if you stayed coaching the line," O'Brien patronized.

He smiled. "Perhaps."

At that moment a waitress in a scant cocktail outfit appeared at the table.

"The gentleman at the bar would like to buy a round of drinks," she said pointing at the man they just left.

"Well, now that's certainly generous," Hollingsworth announced.

He turned in the chair and saluted the man with his drink. Stone, who was facing the beaming man, acknowledged with a polite nod, realizing that it was the celebrated coach's show. O'Brien's back was to him and he didn't turn.

She took the drink orders and left.

Stone noticed a number of glances toward their table as

other important looking people leaned forward to alert their companions of the presence of the famous coach. It felt good to be part of such attention. His thoughts were broken by a question from the college coach to O'Brien.

"Who should we be looking at Saturday?"

O'Brien paused to give the appearance of deep thought.

"Mike of course is our best, but I think four, maybe five more could play for you—O'Halloran, Fisher, Wysek, Battaglia. Collins might be big enough too."

"That many?"

He glanced with a raised brow at Stone who nodded his agreement. He couldn't contradict his boss at such a time. But Collins was a question mark. Wysek, unquestionably a small college prospect. Having played at the major college level himself, Stone wouldn't recommend either to Hollingsworth. The thought reminded Stone that his head coach had played for North Park College, a small college on the north side of the city. Then he immediately felt guilty at the thought. But he hated to think that Hollingsworth might not value his opinion.

"Battaglia, Fisher and O'Halloran are as good a linemen as I've coached." He didn't need to mention Bonjanovich, and Collins and Wysek weren't linemen. He hoped O'Brien wouldn't notice the slight.

"Coach Stone needs to give himself a pat on the back," O'Brien praised. "He's done a great job with those boys."

Stone was taken back by such praise. He had never really been recognized as such by his head coach.

Hollingsworth clucked and tilted his head to the side. "A coach could almost take your entire team and figure on a national championship in four years."

"Well that's probably exaggerating some," O'Brien laughed. "There are a few other players in Chicago to round out something like that."

"That there are, Coach. That there are. But we would be most fortunate to land some of your players."

The waitress appeared with the drinks and asked if they were ready to order.

"Well let's see what we've got," Hollingsworth said opening up a large, expensively looking menu.

"There's an excellent porterhouse in there," O'Brien offered.

"I seem to remember that. It almost puts our Nebraska beef to shame," Hollingsworth said. He carefully scanned the entrees.

"That's what I'll have. Rare."

The two high school coaches ordered the same. When the waitress left, O'Brien excused himself to the men's room, leaving the pair alone.

The college coach watched him weave his way through the tables and then disappear into a hallway. He turned to Jack.

"So Coach Stone, you've got some good boys this year," Hollingsworth said.

Jack found that the great coach had a way of making a person feel like he was the complete center of his attention. He was surprised by how much at ease he was put by him.

"Yeah," he smiled." They're pretty darn good."

Hollingsworth chuckled lightly.

"How about your boy at quarterback?" he asked coyly.

"Bonjanovich? He's a great talent."

"That he is. What do you think about him as an individual?"

Jack became uncomfortable. A few days before the

championship game, he didn't want to disclose how he actually felt about their star quarterback, who was perhaps the finest high school athlete in the country. He thought a few moments.

"I don't know. Mike's a great competitor. He's got his good and bad points like any kid his age, I guess."

He was disappointed with himself for giving such a predictable answer to the question, and then the college coach really put him on the spot.

"I understand he might be in the same trouble as the kid at center. Anything to that?"

"Not that I know of, Coach," he replied warily.

Stone wanted to talk about his linemen. Anyone of the three could play for Hollingsworth, but he didn't seem interested in them. It was obvious that Bonjanovich was the one who peaked his interest, and not these exceptional kids that really deserved much more to be the ones under consideration. And it irked Jack that he had referred to Johnny, who had a name, as 'the boy at center'. He was surprised to suddenly find himself annoyed with the great Owen Hollingsworth, and he wished Coach O'Brien would hustle it up in the john.

The college coach appraised the young man a few moments, and then changed the subject entirely. "Any good movies you might recommend I see while I'm in town?"

CHAPTER 49

After the famous coach had picked up the tab and bid the pair farewell, Frank O'Brien suggested that they go back to the bar for a drink.

"You know Jack, "O'Brien started out, once they were seated, "Coach Hollingsworth is probably the most influential coach in the country. A phone call from him to recommend someone is a guarantee that a coach will get a job."

"That doesn't surprise me."

"He has so much power that I've heard that a word from him can get most any school put on probation."

Jack made a whistling sound for that did seem impressive.

A waitress took their beer orders and then O'Brien leaned across the table and said in a low voice, "We win Saturday and we'll both be in college ball this time next year."

"You think so?"

Excitement returned to the line coach with the thought of getting out of his terrible neighborhood and into the glamour of the college ranks. His earlier disenchantment for Hollingsworth vanished.

"Absolutely."

"If we win big, we might even be talking about a school like Nebraska State."

Pumped by the prospect, Stone boldly stated, "We should win by three or four touchdowns."

"Not without Mike," O'Brien coarsely put in.

The statement stunned him. He had wondered earlier if that

could have been a possibility, but at this late date he hadn't given it a second thought. In Chicago strings were pulled; favors called in. No one with any type of connections would actually end up in serious trouble. He was even surprised that Johnny had been jailed overnight.

"That kid in your class," O'Brien said. "The one that got Costello in trouble."

The drinks had fogged his thoughts and it took a few moments to realize whom he meant.

" You mean Sikorski? Yeah, you asked about him before."

"Right. I want you to talk to him. He could be confused about what he saw."

He stared at his head coach.

"What do you mean?"

He cupped his hands and smiled impatiently.

"This kid could screw up our whole season; all the hours we've put in. Two years for you. More for me. This is our chance to realize our goals. I know that you want into college ball as bad as I do. And you deserve it. You're going to make some college a good line coach. But when Mike leaves, we're back with the rest of the high school coaches, all struggling from week to week. We need to be on top to be considered by the big boys. Look at tonight. You think Owen Hollingsworth's going to take us to dinner next year?"

"But one of the priests said Mike wasn't there. You said so yourself."

He leaned forward and spoke quietly. "Do you believe that?"

Stone shrugged his shoulders and admitted what he had not wanted to. "Probably not."

O'Brien leaned forward. "See what I mean. What if that jackass of a principal we have thinks the same way and decides to keep Mike from playing?"

Stone could see the logic and was becoming more apprehensive with the direction the conversation was taking. He was a little surprised to hear O'Brien use such a harsh word about their principal.

"What do you want me to tell him?" he asked.

"He's a freshman who's probably pretty scared right now with all of this. You tell him he's not sure what he saw. You tell him he's messing up someone's life who has a great future ahead of him. All because he thinks he saw something." He looked around, and then leaned closer. "Tell him he can say whatever he pleases after Saturday."

The waitress brought their beers and O'Brien stretched back until she left. He moved forward again and waited for Jack's reply.

"I don't know coach. How can I do that to the kid?" Stone reluctantly answered. He was still wound up from the apparently real prospect of breaking into college ball and unable to use his best judgment at the moment.

O'Brien opened his palms. "You just do it. It's not a big deal." He looked at his watch. "You better drink up. I didn't realize it was so late." O'Brien stood and laid money on the table to cover the drinks. "This is important, Coach!" he said to his backfield coach and they left.

CHAPTER 50

The next morning Johnny Costello lay atop his made bed with his hands clasped behind his head. Again, he hadn't slept at all during the night and his tired eyes were fixed on the ceiling. The boy hadn't had any problems to speak of in his young life until this. Perhaps he should count the period when he was younger and his dad used to beat him. Then he put a halt to the beatings one night a few years back when he decided to stand up to his father. This sudden show of defiance happened about the time he had made the tryouts for the football team and his dad seemed to now become proud of him. On his wall were sports pennants and pictures of his heroes. A shelf had been constructed to house his trophies. The top of his chest-of-drawers was covered with signed baseballs and footballs, a hockey puck from the Chicago Stadium and tiny sports ornaments of various sorts. His whole life was athletics. He had never considered life without athletics and now, a high school senior, he is at home lying in bed with nothing to do while his teammates are preparing for the day he had dreamed of for so many years. Downstairs, his mother fretted and cried most of the day away. He hadn't seen his dad since his bail bond had been posted. He went to work, and then stayed at the bar until late at night. When he came home to sleep, Johnny would hear him rummaging loudly without any consideration to his family for something to eat downstairs. Then in the morning, he would hear him creep quietly by his door, as if his son had the plague, to wash up. Johnny lay awake through all of this, day and night. He wanted to sleep. He needed it desperately, but he was too tired. He would close his eyes hoping that it would come, but he was also afraid of the nightmares; flames shooting high in the sky or black steel bars with rats running in and out through the spaces. He turned over and put his face into the pillow to try to lock out the terrifying images. Would it be possible to ever sleep again in peace?

CHAPTER 51

Jack Stone hadn't been sleeping fitfully either that night. A sizable weight was heavy on his conscience. The evening before he had thought it would all be quite straightforward. He would tell his head coach what he could do with the college job. But at three in the morning he woke up to gunshots. Half-awake in bed, he listened to sirens scream through the night. Then red flashing lights illuminated his tiny room and he got up. From his window he saw two squad cars turn up a street apparently in chase of the shooters. He was now wide-awake in a cold apartment. The furnace was in need of repair again and it would be a few days before the landlord got it fixed. At his salary Stone had no choice but to live in such a place. A college job would get him out of this, into a nice apartment maybe in a college town like Champaign or West Lafayette or Madison. Or maybe somewhere warm like Phoenix or Baton Rouge. He was in his mid-twenties with a chance he might not see for ten years. Ten years seemed like an eternity to someone his age. It should be easy to tell the kid to keep his mouth shut. Let Bonjanovich have his dreams. It wasn't a big deal. The fire was probably an accident. The kids couldn't be brought back, could they? So why should he feel reluctant to tell the kid to get amnesia? These troublesome early morning thoughts kept Jack Stone awake in a cold apartment with gunfire heard on the street below.

CHAPTER 52

By the next afternoon Johnny Costello had not left his room for nearly two days except to use the bathroom. His mother would bring hot meals up several times a day only to have to pick up the untouched plates from outside his door in tears.

From the time he had confessed in the Malloy conference room a marked decline became apparent in his appearance. His eyes were sunken and red, and his face was unshaven. In a matter of days the boy seemed to have aged well beyond his teens. To him, life no longer had purpose. How could he face any of his friends? And the teachers must think of him as a dope. On several occasions he had passed by the Teacher's Lounge when a door was open and overheard teachers making fun of students. He wondered what they were saying about him now.

Johnny thought back to that morning by Mike's house. Why were they in that prairie? Shouldn't there have been something else for two high school seniors to be doing? Why did they throw stones at that small freshman with blonde hair? And, oh God, why did they sail those shingles where the kids were playing? He felt so reckless and invincible at that time, a member of the greatest team in Malloy history and a friend of the famed Mike Bonjanovich. And then everything changed; though he never realized that it had. After the incident he actually convinced himself that it hadn't happened. Hadn't Mike shrugged it all off? But it had happened. He was put in jail because of it, and now he could hear the sounds of the boys screaming. He remembered the sounds. Young voices shouting out in surprise when the smoldering shingle landed on them. Then that dreadful squeal came from the structure. It must have been when the fire had taken hold. Flames soon after shot up in the air. Johnny wanted to try to help the kids, but Mike said they couldn't. So he didn't. And then they were running up the alley. Mike was right about it being too late. The kids were done for. What could the two of them do except get into trouble by staying? Maybe get booted from the team. It wouldn't bring the kids back. So why do it? But what Johnny had blocked from his thoughts was the knowledge that his quarterback had seemingly took pleasure in the blaze. That laugh. Was Johnny dreaming that he heard it? No, it was real. It was a sinister, criminal act and Johnny couldn't think of it while holding his quarterback in such esteem. So he washed it from his thoughts, as he had eliminated the realization that the heroes of Malloy High School left three boys to burn to death in that barren prairie.

With his face hard into the pillow, which was soaking up tears, he fought against blaming Mike for he was a team player. He had always been a team player. It was the essence of him. The team must win the championship and with Mike the title was a certainty. For the team he must not implicate Mike. He had made the right decision and he must stick by it, even though he was aware of the cruel side of Mike. Then he saw those dull eyes of that man in jail. To spend any more nights as such was inconceivable.

It was then that Johnny began to drift in a dangerous direction. What good could life be without his sports, he thought nearly aloud? It was all he knew and all he was good for. The boy was terribly tired. Fatigue was getting the best of him. He drifted in and out of dreams without actually falling to sleep. Soon he wasn't able to distinguish between the dream world and the realty of the day. It was dark. So dark that he couldn't make out his hand just inches from his face. The air was thick and held an odor of urine. He felt alone laying on something with his back up against a wall, but there was a distinct presence in the blackness. At first he thought it was another person rustling about. Frightened, he called out but there was no answer. The movement stopped for a few moments, then continued. He listened carefully but couldn't quite make the sound out. It seemed to get closer, but it was impossible to tell. Then a flash of light, perhaps it was lightning, momentarily lit up the room. And there it was. Little black pea eyes, just inches from his face, and the chattering of teeth. A large fat rat! In the same light he saw the bars. He screamed. The scream was real as Johnny could still hear it in his bedroom as he broke from the nightmare.

"Johnny?" his mother's frightened voice called out from below.

"It's okay, Ma," Johnny said.

But it wasn't okay. He sat upright on his bed. The room was bright from the afternoon sun and his shirt was soaked through with perspiration. Nightmares used to have an exhilarating effect on him. When he would awake, he could laugh off the horror and feel good about the life to which he had returned. Now he would awake to a real nightmare. Johnny couldn't think clearly. For a moment he thought of Mike. He had all the answers. He would get him out of this. Then he realized how fruitless such a thought was. His first serious thought of suicide came as he remembered his father's hunting rifle downstairs. But his mother was down stairs and would constantly be aware of his presence. That wouldn't do. There were the pills in the bathroom. His mother's sleeping pills. He had heard of how an actress once took her life with sleeping pills and alcohol. Did he need to drink some whiskey also? He was too tired to give it much thought. He sat up in bed. The fatigue was such that his head spun for a moment. He caught his bearings and got up and labored to the bathroom. He saw that the bottle was a third full and, in a surreal state, he washed down the contents and returned to bed.

CHAPTER 53

About the time Johnny Costello was beginning to drift off into a long sleep, Jack Stone was paging through morning *Tribune* in the Teacher's Lounge. He saw the words on the paper, but none were registering. His mind was elsewhere. Soon the bell would ring taking him to his class with the Sikorski kid. Maybe the boy would be sick. Flu season had begun. Maybe he'd be hit by a truck or fall off the bus and break his leg. Stone chuckled aloud at such foolishness and looked around to see a priest at the end of the table look up from his prayers and smile. This was silly. Pretty soon he would be talking to himself.

At that moment he thought of Johnny and wondered how he was doing. With the excitement of the championship on Saturday, he realized uncomfortably that he hadn't spoken to his troubled center since his arrest and decided to give him a call. At first he was angry with the boy that he had let his team down and the coach had no interest in calling Johnny. Then he felt ashamed by such thinking. Johnny wasn't a bright boy, but he wasn't an evil person either. His poor judgment put him into a terrible fix, but hadn't Jack himself made bad decisions in his life? He closed the paper and went to the lounge phone. Stone often called his linemen at home for various team matters and dialed the Costello number from memory.

Mrs. Costello answered wearily but brightened up when she realized who was calling. "Yes, Coach Stone. I'll get Johnny for you." She quickly set the phone down and hurried to get her son. While Stone waited he heard no sounds from the Costello household. No radio music or television. No dog barking or baby crying like he might hear in other homes; just silence.

After a length of time a strange sound came from what seemed to be a good distance from the phone. He couldn't quite make it out, but he became more attentive. Then it came louder and closer. He was sure that it was Mrs. Costello screaming hysterically. Into the receiver she babbled and sobbed and Stone's gut twisted with apprehension, for he sensed what was coming.

"What is it!" he yelled, causing others in the room to turn.

But Tina Costello was completely incoherent. Stone attempted to no avail to calm her down and promptly hung the phone up. Then he dialed the operator and put in an emergency call for an ambulance to be sent to the Costello residence, the address he also knew from memory.

"Father!" Stone yelled hurriedly poking his head into the principal's office. The principal put his hand on the mouthpiece of the phone he had in his hand. "Something bad has happened at Costello's home. I'm going there now. Could you call his father?"

Father Sobykevich excused himself from his phone call and called for Wanda to quickly bring the Costello file.

Stone arrived at the West Side bungalow as two firemen were rolling Johnny on a stretcher from his house to a waiting ambulance. Covers were up to his chin. His head was turned to a side and his eyes were closed as they brought Johnny by his line coach. Respectable distances away from the ambulance were neighboring housewives in their aprons with hands to their mouths. On the small cement porch to the house was

Johnny's mother, standing alone and frightened with her hair in a complete mess.

Stone found out from the ambulance driver where they were taking Johnny, and he went up to the house.

"I can drive you to the hospital, Mrs. Costello."

She wasn't listening to Stone. Instead her watery eyes were on the ambulance that held her dear son. The doors to the long red emergency vehicle were slammed shut and the siren blared loudly as the driver shifted into gear and pulled away from the curb.

"I didn't have another child because Al said we couldn't afford one," Tina said weakly. "We sinned, didn't we? God is punishing me." Her eyes followed the ambulance down the block until it turned a corner. She continued to look at the point where her boy had vanished.

"They're taking Johnny to the hospital," Stone gently beckoned. "I'll take you there. He'll be all right. "

He had no idea of Costello's condition, but he saw that she was in no shape at the moment to hear uncertainty.

She looked around at nothing in particular and then began to shiver.

"We'll go inside to get your coat."

She nodded vacantly and submitted to Stone's direction.

Costello was in the emergency room when they arrived at St. Mary's Hospital. The waiting room was made of marble with a high ceiling and had a strong odor of antiseptic. They were there nearly a half an hour before a doctor came out with any word.

"You're the family of Jonathan Costello?"

Tina nodded slowly with her hand to her mouth, terrified of

what she might hear. Stone got up.

"This is his mother. How is he?"

The doctor looked at Stone a moment, and then said, "He's very sick, but we got his stomach pumped in time. We'll keep him at least overnight to be sure. Maybe longer."

Tina let out a sharp cry and sagged. Stone caught her before she hit the floor. He wasn't sure if she fully understood what the doctor had said.

"Johnny's going to be all right," Stone reassured her and repeated the news until she seemed to comprehend what he was saying. He thanked the doctor and took some standard instructions before helping Tina back to her seat.

"Can I see my son?"

"In awhile," Stone replied. "The doctor said he's asleep now."

She tried to smile at him and Stone thought of hugging her, but then he figured that such a gesture would probably be unfamiliar to this lady.

Ten minutes later Al Costello stormed into the waiting room.

"Where the hell is he?"

The whiskey on his breath hit Stone almost immediately and he got up.

"Johnny's going to be okay," Stone said. "He's with the doctor."

Al looked down at his wife.

"How did you let this happen?" he barked. Loose dentures clicked between every other word.

Tina Costello began to sob pitifully.

Stone flared, but he was able to repress an urge to slap Costello hard against his face. He turned and moved away.

"I just about had him out of this, and it cost me a pretty penny," he shouted, directing his tirade both to his wife and to Stone, as if the coach had something to do with the mess at hand.

"And now look what he does. And I have to hear it from a lousy cop at the park who hears it over his radio. Then the damn priest calls me from school."

Costello paced back and forth intensely, looking down at Tina with contempt.

"The neighbors know. My friends know. Everyone knows!"

He looked at Stone. "And you say he's all right!"

"Yes," he answered tiredly, sick of the elder Costello.

Al continued to pace angrily, and then he stopped and faced Stone.

"The hell he's all right! After all I've done for him." He stopped and turned to his son's coach and said, "Maybe he should have just done it right and killed himself."

Tina let out a dreadful squeal and fell from her chair in a dead faint. Stone raced over and tried to lift her by her fatty arms. A nurse had been close by, listening to Al's tirade, and quickly brought smelling salts to revive Tina. Soon they had her back in the chair with her head down to better regain consciousness.

The nurse took over and Stone went to Johnny's father. He took him by arm and guided him behind a pillar away from Tina's view. He tightened his grip and put his face close to Al's and said with clenched teeth, "Listen you worthless piece of shit, if you talk about Johnny like that anymore and I'll beat you so hard you'll be in here for a month. And I'll beat you twice as bad if hurt your wife."

Costello tried to pull away, but was no match for the powerful hold by the line coach. For a few moments he was submissive, and then he regained his drunken bluster.

"Who the hell do you think you are?" he blurted out with teeth clicking loudly. "You're not much older than Johnny and you think you can talk to me like that you goddamned punk?"

In a swift move Stone gripped him and lifted him at the throat with a powerful hand. Furious, he whispered into Costello's whiskey breath, "You think I'm kidding, huh? Do you understand?"

Costello's eyes began to bulge. His heels were off the floor and Stone's hand was cutting off his air supply.

"I don't hear anything." Stone's teeth were tight and he put further pressure on Al's throat.

Finally Costello made a gurgling sound and nodded. His face was purple. Stone let him go and Al stumbled backward and fell on to the floor. He made no attempt to get up. Stone turned to Tina and saw that she had at least heard some of what went on behind the marble pillar. The look on her face was fearful and pitiful.

"I'm sorry Mrs. Costello. I'm sorry for you and Johnny," he said quietly.

He left them, but before going through the lobby door, he could see in the reflection of the window Tina moving on wobbly legs to attend to her husband.

CHAPTER 54

Unaware of Johnny Costello's suicide attempt, Nick Bonjanovich toyed with a paperweight on his desk as he contemplated the dilemma that could conceivably hurt Mike's chances for the right college deal. Johnny Costello was dumb for sure, but he suspected that the boy knew how to keep his mouth shut. Whatever Frank O'Brien knew was not a concern for the coach needed Mike and wasn't about to foul up this chance at college ball. And Mike had an alibi all right. He was sure that Mike had something on that jackass of a priest, and the cops wouldn't press a priest any more than they might have already. But what about this kid that pointed a finger at Johnny and Mike? He would probably testify against the boys. Nick thought of his friend who had made the offer to solve anything that could hurt Mike. It was only a couple of days to the game and Nick was getting desperate. Nick pressed the weight hard between his palms, and then tossed it to the side of his desk. He opened his desk drawer for the number he needed.

CHAPTER 55

To survive in the jungles of Southeast Asia, John Harnett had learned to maintain focus and plan well in advance. If anything were to happen he felt, it would take place before the Saturday game. And it would somehow involve the muscle Bonjanovich had met at the west side bar.

The early morning weather had warmed enough for a misty, cold rain to fall. Harnett was in his car outside of the apartment of Joe Gatta, the muscle from Stone Park. It was a simple task to trace the man's name and address through his license plate. Gatta was a real pro with a reputation as a vicious mob enforcer. The undercover cop kept his engine off as Gatta would surely spot exhaust from a parked car. Hartnett didn't have to wait long as Gatta stepped from the doorway just as the first light of day was beginning to show. Though a face was hard to recognize at that time of the morning, Harnett couldn't mistake the burly shoulders and the wary scan Gatta automatically made of the neighborhood. The thug blew onto his hands and looked both ways, then stepped onto the sidewalk and went to his car.

Harnett followed in his Chevy at a safe distance. His lights were off. The morning light was such that one could get pulled over for having the headlights off, but Harnett needed to take that chance. They drove west, toward Oak Park.

Fifteen minutes later Gatta pulled into the parking lot of a hotel on River Road and drove through the rows slowly. Harnett drove by and circled back. Across the street was another hotel. He drove into that lot and parked where he could watch Gatta.

Finally, Gatta parked his car and the husky man got out and walked to an older model Pontiac Bonneville. He glanced briefly over each shoulder as he approached it and then fidgeted with the driver's door. Moments later he was inside and tucked down under the dashboard. Soon the engine of the big car started up and he slowly drove it from the lot. Harnett followed, again at a safe distance.

Joe Gatta stopped the stolen car mid-way down a block on a street in Oak Park. There were several cars along the side so Harnett had to park a distance away. His view was good though, even though the gloomy drizzle. He rolled down his window to get a clear picture of the neighborhood and saw that a bus stopped at the end of the block on which the two cars were waiting.

Students were beginning to gather at the stop, and Harnett kept his engine running this time. He became anxious, feeling that something was about to happen and he was further from Gatta than he wanted to be. There were contingencies that bothered him; traffic could box him in and traction was uncertain from the rain. He hadn't slept during the night, but he could deal with that.

A couple of minutes later Harnett saw Gatta's car jerk slightly. He had shifted into gear. It was time to move. The cop pulled out in front of a slow moving car. He feared a horn, but one didn't come. Slowly, he moved down the block, apprehensive that he might have to pass Gatta's car. But that worry was quashed when the Pontiac moved away from the curb about thirty yards in front of Harnett.

The cop gave a quick glance ahead to the bus stop and noticed a boy with blonde hair under a stocking hat apart from the crowd. He might be the Sikorski boy whom the Captain had described. There wasn't much time. He picked up speed and closed the gap when Gatta increased his speed. Sensing what the thug had in mind, Harnett put the petal to the floor hard and the big engine responded. His Chevy lurched forward and gained speed at a compelling rate. It overtook Gatta just as he was turning in toward the blonde kid. The boy wouldn't have a chance. A second thrust edged the Chevy to the lead and Harnett turned hard into the Pontiac.

Gatta's eyes were wide when he turned to see what was suddenly forcing him from his path. They had been trained on the boy. By reflex he started to turn into the other car when he hit a huge oak tree head on. He hadn't had a chance to brace himself and the force sent him through the windshield at a deadly angle.

Harnett, in turn, braked and turned the wheel sharply to the left. His car slid dangerously and then a tire blew causing his Chevy to flip. Children screamed and scattered in all directions as Hartnett's car turned over and over. The Chevy finally came to a dusty and upright halt in the street. It was mangled with shattered windows, but Hartnett survived as he was able to brace himself properly to avoid the same fate as Joe Gatta.

CHAPTER 56

Word of the incident in Oak Park soon reached the principal of Malloy, and Father John spent most of the day sorting out the disturbing details of this near tragedy involving his freshman student. He needed a clear picture of what had happened before any action was to be taken. By early afternoon he had enough information and he went straight to the coaches' office.

"I've got a meeting in two minutes Father," Frank O'Brien said impatiently as he was about to leave the office. The priority of Saturday's game over any other matters was unmistakable in his tone.

"This won't take long, Frank," the principal replied closing the door. "Are we alone?" He looked toward the coaches' locker room.

"Yeah," O'Brien answered with some surprise. "Coach Stone's still in class."

Father John moved away from the door.

"There was an attempt on the life of a student today."

"Really," O'Brien responded, mentally placing the whereabouts of his players during the day. But he quickly dismissed the notion. He felt confident that word would come to him first if one of his players was involved in an accident. Then he realized that the reference was to a deliberate act rather than an accident and he became uneasy.

"There is proof," the principal continued, "that Mike Bonjanovich is connected to this crime."

O'Brien's stomach clenched.

"That can't be."

"I wish that was the case. But it's not."

O'Brien found himself instantly in a panic.

"What proof is there?"

The principal blinked with surprise.

"Mr. O'Brien, this is not a courtroom. I've said that there is proof of his connection. That has to be good enough."

But to O'Brien at this moment it was not good enough for he immediately grasped what would be coming next. The game was set and college scouts from around the country were arriving at O'Hare at this moment.

"That's unacceptable, Father. It's not fair to the boy or to the team. I really need to know what information you have."

The principal removed his glasses and rubbed his eyes. He put them back on and focused on his callous head coach.

"Mr. O'Brien, as of this moment you are no longer the coach of our football team."

O"Brien blurted a laugh.

"That's absurd. You can't do that." Going to his strength, he added, "The Father's Club won't stand for it. They'll have your Polish ass."

"Mr. O'Brien, pick up your personal belongings and get out of my school before I have you arrested."

Father John opened the door and left the office. O'Brien felt an urge to run after him and club him in the back of his wretched head. But he didn't. Instead, he sat down in stunned silence at the desk chair that was no longer his. He couldn't believe that this was happening to him.

CHAPTER 57

"He can't fire you with the championship game on Saturday!" Nick Bonjanovich yelled into the phone.

He listened intently from his desk biting hard into a fingernail. The worst was yet to come.

"What!" he then screamed. "What do you mean he suspended Mike?"

Frank O'Brien started to talk and was cut off.

"Where's Mike now?"

O'Brien didn't know. He'd heard that he had shoved the principal against a locker when he was told of the suspension and left the school.

"I'll take care of this!" Nick shouted and hung up the phone, not giving the football coach time to request his intercession with Father John on behalf of his job.

Nick chewed savagely at his nail. By noon he'd heard about Joe Gatta through his police contacts. He missed the kid. It's probably better that he had. The cops would put out more time and effort for a dead kid. There had to be a tail on Gatta, which meant they knew about him. But he wasn't worried. He'd been in jams with the law before. They didn't have anything on him and Gatta was out of the picture. What concerned him most was Mike. Scholarship Letters of Intent for the major colleges weren't out yet. If Mike was suspended from the big game, there would be plenty of questions asked. Would the top schools then have second thoughts? The renegade schools would come after him like sharks and Nick didn't want that. Television avoided those schools like the plague, as did the big city presses. He'd heard reporters scoff at the upstarts out west. Mike's chances to be an All-American and a top pro pick would be diminished significantly at any of those schools. He had to settle down and think. He worked on the nail some more until a trickle of blood appeared. He decided to place a call to Gus, the college bird-dog who had greased his palm well enough over the year.

"Hello, Nick," the recruiter answered affably.

"Gus we've given the matter a lot of thought. The kid's been under a lot of pressure with the game and everything. He wants to get this off his chest so that he can concentrate on Saturday. Your school is best for Mike. That's where he's going."

After a short hesitation Gus replied with some surprise, "That's good to hear Nick. The staff will be pleased."

"Yeah. One thing. I know the letters don't come out for a few months. We need a guarantee. A signed letter committing to a scholarship. The side stuff doesn't need to be in it of course. Just a guarantee. I can stop by and pick it up today."

"That's something I need approval on, Nick. It might even be illegal to send one out before the official date."

"Illegal?" Bonjanovich blurted out angrily. "You've got to be kidding. What kind of a fool do you take me for?"

"It shouldn't take long to get what you need," Gus said ignoring the remark.

"Are you or are you not going to offer Mike a scholarship? This might be your only chance."

"Nick, you know what we think of Mike. I just need to check on this."

"Bullshit, Gus! You've got the authority. I'm calling you on your offer and you're not living up to it. This can hurt you in Chicago. You call back when you want and we'll see where we're at."

He hung up. There were a number of calls he needed to make. He'd get Mike lined up. They didn't need that fool coach or that principal. He just hoped Mike stayed out of trouble for a few days.

CHAPTER 58

But trouble was indeed looming for Mike at that moment. He was at the lounge on Mannheim with Carol Fishetti. Seated with him at the bar, she lit her own cigarette, afraid that Mike might burn her face. He was muttering obscenities to himself, then downed a shot of bourbon and slid the glass toward the bartender for a refill.

The day bartender, a medium sized man with hard arms and a thin mustache, hesitated before pouring another one for the brooding high school student.

"He can't get away with it!" Mike yelled.

He put the drink down as hard as the one before. The bartender had just opened a racing form when Bonjanovich banged the glass on the bar for more. He glanced at Fishetti who rolled her eyes.

"You better slow down kid," he said as he moved to get the bottle.

Bonjanovich's dark eyes stayed on the bartender awhile then shifted to the girl.

"You think I'm drunk too. Maybe stupid, huh?"

"I don't think anything, Michael. I'm just sitting here."

He snapped the drink back and slammed it on the bar, expecting another.

"That's enough for today," the bartender said quietly.

"Give me another," he demanded.

He shook his head. "Beat it."

The quarterback stood up abruptly, causing his barstool to

fall back and crash on the floor.

"Who the hell do you think you're talking to!"

The bartender said nothing.

Bonjanovich acted as if he might jump over the bar. The bartender did nothing, but he watched quietly from a corner of his eye as he returned to the form.

Seething, Mike stared at him a few moments, then picked up the shot glass and whipped it against a wall. It shattered, spraying glass everywhere. He spit on the floor and tossed a wad of bills across the bar before leaving.

"Boy, he's crazy," the whore said after the door had slammed shut.

"He's an asshole," replied the bartender as he laid the paper down to look for a broom and dustpan.

CHAPTER 59

Rumors had been spreading wildly throughout the afternoon at Malloy though no official word had been given on the suspension of the great quarterback or the firing of Coach O'Brien. By the final period meaningful instruction was virtually impossible. Teachers continuously needed to ask for quiet until they inevitably fell into the conversations.

So when Mike Bonjanovich stormed through the front door into the main hallway toward the end of the day, he became the immediate focus of all within site. A path opened widely as he walked quickly through the hall and down the stairway toward the freshmen lockers. Midway through the basement hall he found the person he was looking for. In his drunken and irrational state of mind, he placed the blame for his problems on Tony Barbini.

Tony had just opened his locker when Bonjanovich came up from behind. The freshman was twirled around and slammed against the locker. He dropped his books and tried to twist from the iron grip pinning him to the locker, but the strength of the great athlete was overpowering. Barbini saw the crazed look in the senior's eyes and smelled the stench of whiskey on his breath.

The punch that Bonjanovich threw was such that it could have crushed Barbini's head against the locker, but the drunken state of the quarterback and a quick shift by the younger boy caused the blow to miss its mark. It did open a slight gash on the Tony's cheek and the locker was smashed inward. Bonjanovich put so much into the punch that Tony was able to slip down and break the grasp. In an instant he was on a dead run through the hall. The boy realized he was no match for the power of the maddened Bonjanovich and he needed to find protection quick.

As drunk as he was Bonjanovich moved along the hall after the freshman with incredible dexterity and speed. He was gaining on the boy when Tony disappeared into the boiler room. The senior followed him into the noisy room, nearly tearing the door from its hinges. There was no sign of Tony as Mike looked in every direction. He hadn't been in this room before and he was unfamiliar with the layout. Equipment churned and steam hissed. The air was hot and rank, but he didn't notice it. He moved quickly to the right keeping an eye on the door to flush him out. He bent under an insulated air duct. His hate for the kid grew with every step. Then he saw movement from the corner of his eye and pounced on Tony as he tried for the door. The freshman was caught and struggled to break free, but the strength of the senior was too great. He dragged the boy backward about the room like he might a rag doll until he came to the boiler. Then he pressed his head against the plate of the blistering furnace and took immense pleasure in Tony's screams. Scorched hair and skin began to give off a putrid odor. But it was more that the senior was after. Sheer loathing had taken over his sense of reason. His powerful and talented hand was at the boy's throat. He closed the vise until Barbini's eyes began to bulge. The kid's neck was strong, but Bonjanovich knew shortly that he would have the best of it. He showed his yellow teeth and turned slightly to the side for leverage when his right shoulder was dealt such a blow that his hand and fingers instantly lost all use. Pain spread immediately from his head to his foot. He shifted to defend himself but another strike put the finishing touch on probably the most gifted shoulder and arm in the country.

Bonjanovich slumped to the floor and saw above him, just before he blacked out, the janitor with a coal shovel set in his hands.

"Ho, ho," Emil Wujcik chuckled as he looked down at Bonjanovich on the floor with a crushed shoulder. "Very important person. Ho, ho."

CHAPTER 60

"Are we going to play Saturday?" Al Wasko, the team's fullback, asked Jack Stone in the coaches' office. Father John had canceled practice for the day, and Frank O'Brien had left the premises.

"I don't know, Al."

He was at his desk while Wasko sat with one cheek on the desk of his former head coach.

Stone smiled tiredly. "It's a mess, isn't it?"

The fullback shook his head in dismay.

"Did you think Mike was capable of doing that?" Stone asked.

"We've all gotten pissed off, I guess," the boy answered, shrugging his shoulders. "But going after that kid the way he did. I just can't figure it."

They were silent awhile, and then Wasko asked, "What do you think will happen to Johnny?"

"It's hard to tell, Al. He doesn't have a lot going for him at home right now. But most important is he's alive. He's got that."

"Yeah, I guess so," Wasko said without conviction.

At that moment the principal came into the office and both stood up. The priest said to the senior, "Allan, I need to speak to your coach."

"Sure, Father," he complied and waved with a limp hand to Jack as he left.

Father John closed the door and took the chair behind the

desk on which Wasko had been sitting. He pointed to Stone's chair and the line coach returned to it.

"Jack, I've always believed that athletics are an integral part of the school's curriculum; a more refined facet of the Physical Education Department, you might say. No different than Drama is to the English Department. But, for some reason, athletics seem to get out of hand from time to time. This shouldn't ever be allowed at any level. But especially in high school, and above all in a religious school as ours. This sort of thing cannot be tolerated. It contradicts all of our teachings and tears at the very moral fiber of our students." He paused, leaning forward with folded hands. Jack wondered if he was actually about to discontinue football at Malloy, let alone to disallow the team from participating in the championship game. "I'll get to the point," he continued. "I want you to be the head coach at Malloy, beginning with the game Saturday. I know you're inexperienced, but you have the ideals I want. What do you say?"

Stone was speechless. Since the news broke regarding Bonjanovich and Coach O'Brien, he had anticipated being let go and had begun to contemplate his future away from Malloy. And he had figured that the game Saturday wouldn't be played. To be offered the head coaching position was a possibility that had never crossed his mind. And then to suddenly be the head coach in the City Championship game was beyond belief. His reaction must have showed.

"This is not a decision I came to lightly," the principal said with a smile. "There will be plenty of criticism, especially if the team loses Saturday. But you'll do just fine. The young men of Malloy High School need a person like you." Then he added with a sly perception, "There'll be a head coaching pay stipend of course. You'll be able to live in a more pleasant neighborhood than the one on Armitage".

Jack realized just how insightful the priest that Frank O'Brien had so maligned was. He felt guilty about his longing to leave Malloy for college ball. Even worse, he felt guilty for nearly telling the Sikorski kid to lie about Bonjanovich. But he hadn't. Had luck intervened with the call to the Costello home? Might he have actually asked Sikorski to lie? It didn't matter, because he hadn't done it, and that was that.

"Sure, Father," he answered straight away. "I appreciate your faith in me. I'll do a good job for Malloy."

"Yes, you will Jack."

They stood and shook hands.

CHAPTER 61

In the Barbini den enjoying warm Holiday drinks were the Sikorskis, the Barbini family and Susan Callaghan. Drinking hot cider, the teen-agers centered about Mary Margaret who was in an exceptional mood. At a mini-bar in a corner sat the two men with Tom & Jerrys while Eileen Barbini stood in the doorway to the kitchen. Wearing an apron with her arms folded, her face was bright from the special mix she normally prepared for herself on such an occasion.

"How do you like our friends, Mary Margaret?" Tony asked his sister, squatting down in front of her.

She gleefully banged at the arm braces on her chair. Susan stepped forward with a small package wrapped with Christmas paper and set it on a table beside her.

"This is for you on Christmas, Mary Margaret," she said and kissed her on the cheek. Mary Margaret responded excitedly.

"I didn't bring a gift, Mary Margaret," Andrew smiled with his hands clasped in front, "But I do want to wish you a very Merry Christmas also."

She reacted again.

"Mary Margaret wishes both of you a Merry Christmas," Tony said with his head turned back up toward his friends.

At the bar Thomas Sikorski watched the exchanges with a sense of comfort. For the first time in years he felt as such. It was good to see his son happy and at ease, and it was pleasant to enjoy a good drink in the warmth of this house.

"Yes, Tom," Jack Barbini said, returning to the conversation they were having before they has paused to listen to the kids. "Three years in the Philippines was enough for me. I was glad that you guys came up with the bomb." Then he winked at his wife. "And besides, Eileen was about to give up waiting for me."

"Fat chance!" she cracked smartly from the doorway with a cigarette dangling from her mouth.

Tom smiled and brought out a pipe from his coat jacket pocket.

"Mind?" he asked Jack.

"Not at all, Tom. Not at all. Next best thing to a good cigar is a good pipe, I've always said."

Jack reached to his box on the bar and bit off the end of a fat cigar. He lit Tom's pipe first with a lighter and then the cigar. Soon both were going nicely, creating a heavy cloud of blue smoke above the bar. Jack raised his Holiday mug to toast.

"He who does not relish wine, women and song, remains a fool his life long."

"For God's sake, Jack, the children!" his wife admonished him.

Their children snickered and Mary Margaret banged at the chair rowdily and Tom Sikorski laughed aloud. His laughter continued and became irrepressible, causing the others to spontaneously join him and the small den was consumed with the joy of life in this wonderful Season.

THE END